Queen Solomon

Tamara Faith Berger

Coach House Books | Toronto

first edition

Canada Council   Conseil des Arts
for the Arts   du Canada

ONTARIO ARTS COUNCIL
CONSEIL DES ARTS DE L'ONTARIO
an Ontario government agency
un organisme du gouvernement de l'Ontario

Published with the generous assistance of the Canada Council for the Arts and
the Ontario Arts Council.

LIBRARY AND ARCHIVES CANADA CATALOGUING IN PUBLICATION

Berger, Tamara Faith, author
      Queen Solomon / Tamara Faith Berger.

Issued also in electronic formats.
ISBN 978-1-55245-372-8 (softcover).

      I. Title.

PS8553.E6743Q44 2018   C813'.6   C2018-903941-8
                                               C2018-903942-6

Queen Solomon is available as an ebook: ISBN 978 1 77056 565 4 (EPUB), ISBN 978
1 77056 566 1 (PDF)

Purchase of the print version of this book entitles you to a free digital copy. To
claim your ebook of this title, please email sales@chbooks.com with proof of
purchase. (Coach House Books reserves the right to terminate the free digital
download offer at any time.)

I, so and so, one of the lowliest,
have probed my heart for ways of grace.
— Abraham Abulafia

Past

She came back for me the first Monday in March, the day that I quit school for good. It had been almost seven years since she'd left. Now she stood on our porch buzz cut, draped in fur, with some middle-aged, square-jawed fuck toy beside her.

'Long time, bruh,' she said. 'This is Christof. From France.'

He was at least fifty, long hair, with grooves in his forehead. With no hair she looked gaunt, more severe than before. 'Can't we come in?' Her gaze fixed right through me.

Under the light of the porch, her eyes had that same telltale sheen. Tongue-tied, I could not acknowledge either him or her again.

Then the guy took off one glove and held out his hand for me. It had this strange, metallic, free-floating warmth. Then he set that same palm on the back of her neck. Barbra moaned just a little, as if it was hot. Her lips were sun-cracked. My mouth lost its spit. I thought she was back here to mock me again.

'How's tricks? How's your dad?' Barbra seemed nervous and grinned.

'Okay and okay.' I felt myself spin. I half-blocked the doorway, gut roiling. *My dad is not the bank machine.*

'What?' Barbra asked, still smiling right through me. 'What'd I do? What'd I do?'

I remembered those teeth, light-speckled and ridged. I stepped backwards too fast, discombobulated.

Then, unrestricted, Barbra shifted herself sideways and just pushed in right past me. Her little French fuck toy followed suit. He dragged some duffle bag in, kicked it up against the wall. Air from outside formed a bubble around me. I watched Barbra hand him her matted fur coat. I watched him slide open our mirrored front closet. Cold sweat had flattened the shirt on my back.

My voice came out hoarse. 'No free hangers in there.'

Barbra laughed for some reason. I smelled like rye bread. The guy dumped both their coats on the slumped duffle bag. He wore army pants and a peasant blouse. Then he bowed at me weirdly before traipsing down our hallway toward the john.

I turned and stared at her, fucking perplexed. 'You gonna tell me what in *God's name* you're doing here again?'

I sounded just like my father. Why was she back in our house with that middle-aged *shyster*?

Barbra tried not to keep smiling, sucking in her bottom lip. She stared at Abigail's drawings in the front hallway, the new ones that had just been framed.

'These are good,' she said coyly. 'She's gotten really, really good.'

Brazen, avoidant, that same gruff tickling voice. Did she actually think she could just be reinstated?

'We came from Peru,' Barbra said. 'This is just a pit stop, all right?'

My blood pumped too fast. Surprise, no surprise. *You already came and you conquered, bitch. Do not come back.*

'Hey. Relax, bruh. Why don't you chill out a bit?'

I stress-checked my phone. My girlfriend was going to be here too soon. Barbra and Ariane were going to meet. God, there was nothing I could do about this now.

For seven years, I'd been trying to deal with myself in this world. I'd thought that graduate school was going to do that for me. I'd thought that reading book after book and then writing a thesis was going to sweep all my thoughts into actions at the very least. I was *wrong*. I still lived at home with my father. School had not carved my fucking problems out of me. Because I had this original problem, the origin of all my problems: Barbra, the leghold trap in our basement. Barbra the Israeli who infiltrated our house for eight fucked weeks when I was sixteen.

My fundamental problem: I turned Hebrew, fractious.

My whole entire head: five-fingered, forked.

I sensed the shyster roaming around somewhere behind me. Her breasts were still massive. I smelled her beef-stock armpits. She wore this weird, rose-coloured, silky potato-sack dress. Striped stockings. Buzzed hair. I wanted to touch her. That pinkish sack dress made her look like an inmate.

'This place hasn't changed one bit, not at all.'

My father was the one who had brought Barbra here. *I was the one who made the bitch bloom. Bloom* is not the right word, but it's what I use for a molester.

I was still living at home after seven fucking years when I should've been in the US like my sister, who was winning genius awards.

The shyster reappeared at her side. He clamped his hand back on her neck. Her shorn head tipped backwards. She moaned freer and shivered. I know white men think they master the universe like this.

§

There used to be a building near our house where women sat on green-painted benches in a small cement courtyard behind a buckling ten-foot-tall fence. Those women watched their kids play on a set of rusted monkey bars. My mother told me that the building was for victims of domestic abuse.

'When a man hits the woman he lives with,' my mother said, 'it's called *domestic abuse*. Being here means that the women have left their abusive situations.'

I remember trying to imagine exactly what the men did to those women who were smoking with each other on the benches behind the fence. Why did their clothes look too big or too tight? Why was the building rundown? Why didn't their kids go to school? I imagined a knock-kneed kick from a man in a suit and one of those women writhing on a kitchen floor. I imagined her raggedy nightdress and a purple eye socket. God, it was disturbing. All their kids on the monkey bars, screaming. I saw flour bags exploding. Sex by the man in a suit. His belt out and pants down, smothering her.

I would never hit a girl, I promised myself when I was ten.

But when Jessie Yung in Grade 6 said that my breath smelled like cat food, I wanted to punch her in the gut.

And once, in Grade 8, I touched Mia Greenwald through her T-shirt while she was passed out drunk on Joel's basement couch. I knew that was abuse, domestic abuse.

Sometimes I hated my sister, too, when we were kids. I hated her so-called special needs. I knew there was actually nothing wrong with Abigail when everyone treated her so carefully.

As I grew up, I think this is what happened: there was something that bothered me in general about girls. It was how they sometimes acted dainty and sometimes crude – even in the same sentence – and no one called them on it. They were two-faced, I'm saying, they herded together. Sometimes I wanted to enter their groups and make space for myself so that they couldn't so flippantly lord their duplicity.

It was not my mother who pinpointed this tendency in me. The Israeli bitch found it and used it immediately.

§

My father put her headshot on the fridge about one month before she arrived. It was an old-looking, folded, passport-sized shot, black and white, with a camera flash flicker lodged in one of her eyes. She had frizzy black hair bobby-pinned slick on one side. Tiny, mottled, square-shaped teeth and doe eyes like a caricature.

'Naive,' said my mother to my father. 'That's a woman, not a kid.'

'Ruth, you of all people should understand,' my father said. 'She doesn't have a family. Her family let her go when she was *five*. She's been in Israel without her family for *years*.'

'We learn to place kids within their communities,' my mother said.

'Come on, where the hell do you suggest they should've "placed" her? There are no Jews left in Ethiopia, Ruth! We had Operation Moses and Solomon for that. We are trying to help orphans get a handle on their lives.'

'Orphans,' my mother snorted.

My mother was finishing her Master of social work. 'I'm not sure your "team" is using the right word.'

My father said that he fought to sponsor *this* exchange student, a *Jewish* one from Israel, a Jewish student who *needed* it. My father always repeated that he was the only Jewish member of his Rotary Club. My mother thought the Rotary Club was sexist. My father said that my mother didn't know what she was talking about.

'That girl was *transferred* to Israel by the military,' said my mom, 'when Israel had no long-term plan for integration. It's a total disaster. Look at Tel Aviv. It's all *white*. It's for whites. They *abducted* the Yemenis, too. Israel has absolutely no framework for understanding race.'

'Jesus Christ, Ruth. These people are *Jews* – not Black people who are offended by the colour white,' my father yelled. He turned to me. 'Tell your mother, Israel *always* has a plan.'

Before I met Barbra, I was kind of on my dad's side.

'I am not cooking for this person I don't even know,' my mother told my father on the day she was set to arrive.

'Social work, Ruth? Sometimes I don't know about your compassion.'

Me and Abigail were watching *America's Next Top Model* in the family room. Fatima was getting her photo taken on a dairy farm in short shorts and a USA crop top. Fatima had just confessed to Tyra Banks that she had been circumcised when she was a kid.

'Clitoridectomy is the removal of the *clitoris*,' Tyra Banks explained to the other models, glossy-eyed, holding Fatima's hand. 'Because they don't want a beautiful woman like this to be free!'

There was no way Abigail understood all of this. She was glued to the screen, mouth-breathing. Fatima broke down in tears on a haystack. Tyra bent over, hugging her, crying, too.

I walked up the stairs to the kitchen, my back wet with sweat. Even in a heat wave, my mother wouldn't turn on the AC.

'Passive-aggressive,' my father said, glancing at me. He was holding the Windex and had a dishtowel over his shoulder. 'Your mother is very passive-aggressive.'

'He thinks I can write off this whole summer,' my mother said to herself.

My father sprayed the lowest part of the fridge around the grates. 'I thought your mother would be happy that an Israeli is not in the army,' he said.

'She can't live in that country if she doesn't finish her bloody tour.'

'The girls don't do "tours," for God's sake, Ruth.'

'Right. They just deal with the trauma of the boys.'

'Listen to her, *trauma*. What do they teach you at that place?'

'You mean the fucking *University* of *Toronto*?'

'Listen to how you're talking in front of your son.'

'What comes out of my mouth is my choice, for fuck's sake.'

'*Again*. Oh my God.'

Both of them exaggerated whenever they got in a fight. I'd call it melodrama but that wouldn't be exact. Their fights were more like the slapstick of lapsed communication. My father had wanted to pick Barbra up at the airport with all of us. He said he wanted it to be a *family affair*. My mother said my father didn't need to involve all of us any more than he already had in his *saviour fantasy*.

I thought, the saviour fantasy is a family affair.

My father had made up a bedroom for Barbra in the basement even though we had a spare room upstairs. 'An eighteen-year-old needs *privacy*,' my father said. He set up Barbra's makeshift room – a box spring and mattress surrounded by curtains, a bar fridge, and a bridge table with a shitty computer – right where me and Joel played *Reaper of Souls*.

'I want to have the house presentable for this girl and it'd be nice if you would all *help* me,' my father shouted as he picked at the bottom of the fridge.

'Shhhhaaa!' yelled Abigail from the family room.

My mother swiped her phone.

My father found some kind of hairball in the fridge grate. He put it on the counter in front of my mother. 'What's this?'

My mother frowned and kept staring at her phone. 'A piece of *shmutz*.'

'This girl is coming all the way from Israel – don't swear at me, Ruth – and she's going to have nothing to eat.'

My mother threw her phone in her purse and got on her jean jacket. 'A house produces *shmutz*.'

'You are not a martyr, Ruth. Don't act like a bloody martyr.'

My mother laughed. 'Why don't you tell me how you really feel?'

Then my mother whipped open the pantry door so hard that it hit the wall.

'Stop making noise!' screamed Abigail.

'You're making your daughter upset.'

'I'm making bloody tuna.'

My mother jerked around the kitchen, leaving cupboards and drawers open as my father kept spraying and wiping the fridge. My mother slit two cans of fish, whipped the tops into the sink. She'd been applying for teaching jobs for the last six months but she hadn't heard back yet. My mother usually made tuna salad with celery and pickles. I watched her dump way too much mayonnaise into a bowl. Then she heaped clumps of the gunk onto pumpernickel bread.

'You'd better not make this girl feel uncomfortable,' my father said.

My mother smashed a bunch of bread together and wrapped the sandwiches in plastic. 'Don't worry. She's all yours. I'm going to a film.'

'Stop it!' said Abigail from the other room.

'Tell your sister where I am,' my mother said to me on her way out. My father slammed the fridge door and went after my mother.

I walked back down to the family room. Fatima, pink-eyed, now posed in a fluorescent green bikini beside a horse who nosed her right between the thighs.

'God, this show is really fucked up.'

'I love *Fatima*,' whispered Abigail.

The phone rang once upstairs. The TV was too loud. I sat down beside my sister who was sucking her fingers. Why was my father so obsessed with the food? Why was my mother acting so angry? I thought, maybe she just didn't want to take care of another kid? I mean, she didn't need to take care of me anymore, but Abigail, even at eleven years old, was work. And my mother was always writing for school now, doing work.

I let Abigail put her feet on my lap. I thought the headshot on the fridge would not want even to eat dinner. I thought she'd be jet-lagged. She'd want to go straight to sleep.

I had just started *The Metamorphosis*. Gregor the cockroach fell off his own bed. I thought I'd tell my dad we should just order pizza or something – tuna fish on pumpernickel was way too specific. That girl probably hated tuna. I thought we should just ask her what *she* wanted to eat.

I heard my father pounding down the stairs. 'Two hours!' he yelled before he left through the front door.

I was thinking of my mother in the theatre alone. She was probably so mad because my father seemed so concerned about this one Ethiopian-Israeli orphan. It's true that he seemed to have these weirdly elaborate plans for her – making bedrooms, cleaning up, planning outings and visas – when he didn't ever seem to be doing that kind of extra stuff for us.

After two more episodes of *America's Next Top Model*, me and Abigail heard my father's car in the driveway. The trunk slammed. Abigail quickly turned off the TV. Gregor Samsa was taken care of by his sister, initially. Abigail was pretty squeamish. I couldn't ever imagine her being nurselike with me.

'I hope I like her,' whispered Abigail, bouncing both her knees.

Grete was the only one who ever accepted Gregor as a bug.

'This is where the kids put their shoes, *na'alayim*.'

I cringed. My father was trotting out his Hebrew.

Abigail jumped up off the couch then abruptly sat down again, jamming her head onto her knees, smothering nervous laughter.

My father kept speaking extra loud and extra slow. 'Can I take your coat, your *me'il*? No? *Lo*? Okay, keep it on, but it's hot today, right? This is where we hang our *me'ilim*. It's going to be a wet summer this year, so you're lucky we've got an extra raincoat – *me'il, me'il geshum*, right? Sometimes it rains here even in the summer. Don't worry if you don't have a cooler *me'il*. Ruth will lend you one of hers, or we can get you a new one because you're not the same size.'

My father laughed. God, it was embarrassing. Abigail, for some reason, punched me in the arm.

'You ate on the flight, *ken*?'

My father was now in the kitchen. Me and Abigail stayed in the family room. The doe-eyed headshot had not said a word.

'The weather's not bad here,' my father rambled, 'but the traffic is *ayom*. Dreadful! I'm sure you have bad traffic in Israel, too, of course.'

God, was this my father acting like the saviour?

'Do you want to sit down, Barbra? *H'bayit shli, oo h'bayit shlach*. My home is your home.'

Fuck. I bet he'd practised that.

I stood up. Abigail kicked the back of my knee.

'Don't!' she hissed.

I tiptoed up the half-staircase toward the kitchen.

'Hungry, Barbra? *At re'eva?*'

My ears got plugged with a rapid heartbeat. A six-foot-tall woman loomed over my father. I only saw her from behind. Maybe my mother was right. My father, multi-armed, waved the bundle of my mother's tuna fish. The woman had shiny black hair slicked back into a bun and a puffy black plastic bomber jacket. I thought of duct tape. Female boxing. A giantess.

'*At re'eva?* You understand?'

I *knew* she spoke English, my dad said she spoke fine.

My father, undaunted, unwrapped the plastic and bit off a hunk of black bread smeared with fish.

'We're going to get you set up so you can rest. *Yashen, shluf.*'

I could hear the cracking in my father's jaw. He could not stand still or stop talking in front of this giant.

Suddenly, Abigail scampered past me out of the family room. The six-foot-tall headshot spun around. She had this big blue vein in the middle her forehead, a pushed-out lower lip. Her face in real life was more amazing than any model.

'I'm Abbi,' my sister said. 'That knob there is my bro.'

I could not believe Abigail was not afraid. My father chucked out his crusts. I leaned against the doorway and nodded in her direction. I started breathing too fast. I had cramps in my gut.

'Are you going to babysit me?' Abigail asked, fawning.

'We're not going to make you work here, don't worry,' my father interrupted. 'Come sit, guys, come eat. This is a meal. We should eat.'

'Drink,' said the headshot. She had a gruff Hebrew voice.

'Of course! I'm sorry,' my father said. 'We have pop in the basement, juice, seltzer, anything you like.'

'I will take wine.'

Abigail giggled. She was actually holding Barbra's hand.

'Okay, okay, we let the kids have wine. We think kids should definitely try a little wine.'

My father retreated to the pantry. That was not where we kept wine. I slowly picked my body off the wall. I felt a sweat-soaked shell on my back.

'Do you like *America's Next Top Model*?' Abigail asked as she led Barbra down to the family room.

My spine creaked to one side. My father shot around the kitchen with a corkscrew. From the kitchen I could see the family room. I realized that my father had totally, absolutely fucked something up. Who was this woman in our house? Why was she here? The Rotary Club was a *men's* charity. She was staying the whole summer. What was their mandate? God, my mother was right. This was a real problem. That was a woman, not a kid. Charity made men feel proud. This was not charity. Charity was simple. There was a ten-foot-tall orphan now lodged in our house.

From the kitchen I watched her unzip her puffy jacket. She crashed down, bouncing, wide-legged on the couch. She had on a peasant blouse with tassels. Sweat-stained armpits.

The biggest tits I had ever seen. They were like bells behind curtains. Tremulous.

Abigail turned the TV back on. She gave the remote control to Barbra. It was judgment time. On *America's Next Top Model*, Fatima was getting eliminated.

I wanted her to look at those models and feel me behind her soaring, peering, overhead.

§

The second night, my mother drank wine with Barbra. We were having takeout Szechuan food.

'Illegal. Stop it,' my father said under his breath.

'You're eighteen, correct?' My mother smiled as she topped up Barbra's second glass. 'Wine is good for your heart.'

Barbra smiled at my mother, teeth crimson. Abigail liked to use her hands to eat. My father talked non-stop about the Rotary Club, saying that at their next meeting he would be bringing up the issue of extending Barbra's student visa, which would allow her to finish her high school diploma here and even start college while living with us.

I looked at my mother. She was glugging her wine. My dad said that Barbra would have to talk to the guys about raising funds for her tuition, but he could talk to Bill Cunningham about the details because Bill was on the board. My father made this stuff sound like a business deal.

'Does it not depend on what *Barbra* wants to study here?' my mother interjected, glaring at my dad. 'Assuming, in fact, that she *wants* to stay?' Then my mother shifted her gaze back to Barbra. 'Tell him. Tell him what you want to study.'

'Just a second there, Ruth…'

'Political literature,' Barbra said slowly, gruffly.

'On the international stage,' added my mother.

I was totally confused. Like, when had my mother and Barbra already had a private conversation? And what did she mean by *political literature*?

My mother smiled falsely at my father, as if she were proving some kind of point. 'Israel is not known for its *diversity* in this department.'

I cringed. *Diversity*. Why would my mother say that word? But my mother and Barbra started laughing for some reason. It was weird. How was diversity in literature or political literature relevant to fucking *anything* right now?

'Israel is a leader, of course, in the tech sector,' my father said, looking back and forth between Barbra and my mom. '3-D animation and the like.'

I watched Abigail finish up her bowl of noodles with two fingers.

'Drones,' my mother said, pouring herself another glass of wine.

'Ruth, that's *enough*,' my father snapped as my mother topped up Barbra's glass.

Barbra hiccupped, glossy-eyed. Kafka was international political literature.

My mother stood up suddenly, holding the rest of the bottle. 'Don't listen to him,' she said to Barbra. 'You can do anything you want to.' Then, to my father: 'You can't tell me what to do.'

'You guys. This is embarrassing,' I said.

'Sorry,' my father said, staring at Barbra.

'Ditto,' said my mother as she gave me a weird nod and left with the wine dregs.

My mother had been drinking way more than normal, it seemed. I wanted to tell Barbra all the ways in which my parents hated each other.

'Lots of leftovers,' said my father, staring at the drenched Styrofoam containers.

Abigail licked her lips clean of sauce. Barbra slurped her last bit of wine.

'Use a napkin,' my father spat. 'Come on, Abigail. You're too old for this.'

I couldn't look directly at Barbra. She actually wanted to study literature here? She was eighteen years old. I knew that kids in Israel at eighteen all went straight to the army. Or maybe they'd already done a year of the army? I actually couldn't imagine Barbra in high school. I literally could not imagine her sitting at a desk. I couldn't imagine her with a gun either. She was a fucking giant. She would distract the whole squad. Her sweat stains would discombobulate them.

'Abigail, stop!' my father yelled, stacking the takeout containers, ruining the remains.

'Just let her wipe her face how she wants to,' I said.

'Barbra, wanna come up to my room now?' Abigail said. She ignored my dad and talked to Barbra exactly like I wished I could.

My legs burned. She was now staring at *me*. It felt like, for a moment, she knew what I was thinking. What *was* I thinking? That she was lax in the mind? That our table was lopsided from the weight of her tits? That was fucked. I was fucked. My parents were fucked.

All of a sudden, I felt illiterate.

As if this orphan from Israel was mind-murdering me.

My father would say, *Stop exaggerating! Everything in you is exaggeration.*

But I felt like the hole had already been dug. I sat at the table with my feet staked in muck.

§

One night later, I finished *The Metamorphosis*. I'd started on *Letter to the Father* when I heard a scratch at the door. It was two a.m.

'Go back to bed,' I whispered. 'Put on your headphones.'

Abigail sometimes came to my room if she woke up in the middle of the night.

Letter to the Father, I realized, solidified the thesis about Kafka that he was repressed by his dad.

It is as if a person were a prisoner, Kafka wrote in the letter about living in his father's home, *and he had not only the intention to escape but the intention to rebuild the prison as a pleasure dome.*

It occurred to me, too, that that was what the cockroach was – this kind of entrapment *and* a way to feel pleasure: an attempt to escape the pain in your head and transfer it down the tracks of your body. Kafka felt that his father kept him in a kind of a prison when all he really wanted was his father's confidence or conviction – or whatever it was – to be smoothly, pleasurably passed down to him limb to limb.

I heard another scratch.

'Oh God, just come *in*.'

Kafka did not want his father's cruelty in him.

My door opened. It was *her*. Not my sister. No definable expression. Her T-shirt hung like a dress to her knees.

'What?' I said, immediately paranoid.

Barbra leaned back against my door. The door clicked.

'What?' I repeated.

I could not move. I mean, not even a fraction. Not even in my mind.

Six feet. I'd smelled her since she'd been in our house: mushrooms, beef stock, cigarettes. She *smoked*. I felt my book getting droopy, a pain in my thumb. She just stood there and stared at the diamond-shaped fixture on my ceiling. Her nipples showed through the T-shirt like shadows. She wasn't wearing pants. Her tits were vegetal, amorphous. Black pine-needle hairs stuck wet down both sides of her neck.

'Are you okay?' I said, trying to keep the book up in my hand.

Criss-cross thatches showed through the white T-shirt. What was she doing half-naked? I could see *pubic hairs*.

'You can't sleep?' I squeaked. God, I had to get up. My father would be shocked if he knew she was here.

I had a single bed right under the window. Our house was two floors. Maybe the basement was cold. Maybe bleach was the problem, maybe that stench in the pipes. Maybe that was why she was up here in my room: it was technical. She did not look me in the eyes.

Barbra suddenly pitched herself forward, legs folding funny at the knees.

On my bed, she lay down.

I stood up quickly. I yawned.

'Scratch my back, bruh,' Barbra said.

She turned her back to me, facing the wall. Her T-shirt was long. Her bare tits stacked under there. Who was *bruh*? What was *bruh*? I kept yawning and yawning. I could not see the future of this summer. This orphan with no underwear took up my whole bed. Six feet, wooden legs. I didn't know what to do. I watched, I just stood there, as she somehow lifted up her T-shirt and tucked it around both her shoulders like a drape. She exposed her whole back. It was curved and marked up with these bruiselike polka dots. What were those marks? She *was* wearing panties. They were nearly see-through, like a window screen.

'Scratch,' Barbra said. Her voice was Hebrew, vibrating.

I dropped my book on the floor. Her shirt only covered her tits. She had ribs like a humpback, flesh rolls at her waist.

'Scratch my back,' she repeated.

Was she allergic to something? Was she allergic to us?

I'll tear you apart like a fish, Kafka's father said.

Bird's-eye, my hands looked so measly and pink. Jews are threatened by threats, I read that somewhere. I finally sat back down on my own bed. Heat drummed off her back. Those were pockmarks, maybe burns. Vibrating itch.

'If you don't scratch,' Barbra said, 'I feel like I could scream.'

I used my cold nails. I did it.

'Harder,' said Barbra, arching, relieved.

I scratched the board of her back until white lines appeared. My nails were short. It felt good to scratch her. I felt it in my gut, in my cock, I felt scratching everywhere. The criss-crosses I made turned into red notches. I thought, I could never let her see my hard cock. I thought of a worm on the sidewalk in the rain. Sweat streaked down one side of my face. I scratched even harder between her shoulder blades.

Then Barbra suddenly rolled over, untucking her shirt and immediately re-covering herself down to her knees. She looked at me, smiling. I'd seen the bottoms of her tits.

Her hair formed a stiff open fan on my pillow. Her teeth were wine-stained.

'Thanks, bruh,' she said. 'You're good at that.'

I felt the pull of the street light outside. I knew that this person was asking something from me, this stranger in my room on my bed. Her tits were slack under her T-shirt. I wanted to touch them. I knew that I couldn't. I had just scratched her back. Did she want a new family? A brother? Is that what *bruh* means?

'Put your hand in my head,' Barbra said.

I knew she meant hair, put your hand in my hair. Maybe she wanted me to scratch her there next? All of a sudden, it occurred to me: *don't*. This person in your room is an actress-in-training. An actress-in-training who has weird little teeth – like bird's eggs, sort of speckled.

'C'mon, do it,' the actress whispered at me.

My heart sped up as if it was rigged. I didn't know what she wanted. I wanted to touch her mushrooming tits but that was not what she just asked for. I reached out in slow motion. My fingers felt shrivelled. I would do what she asked for. I put my hand first at the side of her head. It felt starchy. I dug in. I didn't think.

'Lift up now,' she said.

I felt my neck tense. Barbra closed both her eyes. I had to grab her hair to lift her up like she asked for. Her hairs twisted round my knuckles that were big and strained white. I pulled from the roots. My cock started pulsing so hard that it hurt.

'Higher,' she said.

I took her head up by the hair so it cleared the whole pillow. Her hairs threaded through my knuckles; they wound around my thumb. It was easy. She smiled. I *would* show her my cock. Yeah, she would see how my cock could explode. I jerked her up by one side. She kept smiling. She liked it. I was hardened all over, like concrete, no cracks.

All of a sudden, Barbra opened her eyes wide. 'In Israel, bruh, they treat us like dogs.'

I dropped her. She squealed. I covered her mouth. I tried to unwrap my fingers of all her hair. My parents were *sleeping*. Barbra pushed my hand off her mouth.

'Stop,' she hissed.

'*Sorry.*'

'You racist?' she said.

What? Did she mean because she was Black? Because I'd dropped her? *What? Who* in Israel treated Barbra like a dog? Barbra started to hiccup. I was scared that she might vomit. This person was *drunk*. My father said she was an orphan, abandoned when she was five. I wasn't racist. Jews can't be racist. People all over the whole world hate Jews. I didn't understand. Israel *rescued* the Ethiopian Jews. 'The Ethiopian Jews are *lucky* to be in Israel!' my father said. 'The army transferred more than *fourteen thousand* Jews in less than two days!'

Pressing the wall, Barbra tried to sit up and move to the side of my bed.

'Can I sleep up here tonight?' she whispered.

The hairs raised on my arms. 'Not a good idea.'

Suddenly, Barbra launched herself forward. I realized she was going to be sick. There was cud in her cheeks. It looked like she had to spit. I'd just scratched her back and she hated me now. She called me a *racist*. *Was* I a racist? Barbra toppled toward my door, reaching out for a wall.

'*Wait*,' I said.

In one single-armed sweep, Barbra took off her T-shirt. Her back was a graph of welts that I'd made.

I heard Barbra pounding down two flights of stairs. I thought my parents would both for sure wake up. I was afraid of my father finding out she'd been here.

I scuttled over to her T-shirt. The wrinkles exuded her musk. I felt myself spinning so fast, like this was not my room, like I was not on the carpet, like I was not even there.

I thought, I can't touch this person *ever again*.

§

Two years ago, in Grade 10, Joel took me to a party near his cottage where some really short girl with dyed black hair said she would suck me if I gave her the rest of my flask. Joel said, 'Yo, bro, it's your lucky day.' He said, 'Yolanda's a slut.' I told Joel to fuck off. I knew that was stupid. Joel always called girls *bitch* and *slut*. I thought calling a girl *slut* was a totally abstract insult. And that wasn't even from my mother. *Slut* just sounded amphibian to me.

I followed Yolanda into a bathroom in the basement. She had white flecks in her scalp, a rigid part line. The bathroom had mint-coloured tiles and an old deer-legged sink.

'Sorry,' Yolanda said, showing me her tongue. 'I might be out of commish.'

There was a stud in there, stuck, a metallic cyst. A little vomit-taste flowered the back of my tongue. I held out my flask for her. She took a long swig.

No one had ever sucked me before. Joel knew that. He knew it.

'Getting numb now, thanks, man,' Yolanda said as she drank the JB we'd pilfered from Joel's dad.

'You don't have to.' I shrugged.

'I actually just want to see if it hurts.'

Then Yolanda went down on her knees. She went down by herself. Pimples frothed under her dusted pink cheeks. Then she yawned and I quickly unzipped my jeans. My cock bounced right into her chin. Then she just put her hand around it, like grabbing it, and I was suddenly inside her mouth. It felt like she was flogging the side of my cock with her tongue. It felt hard. It felt amazing, like a tickle, like a wrestle. I forgot all about her silver cyst. I put one hand on her head, one hand on the sink. Hot spit churned in her cheeks. It occurred to me that she *liked* this. This girl I'd never met before *liked* sucking me. She clamped my cock without her teeth. I didn't know how she did that. She seemed greedy to feed. Her lips felt like tightening rubber elastics. Then this fucking incredible washing-machine suction churned up from my balls and I spewed right inside of her. It felt endless. I swear I blacked out for a second.

Then I heard water running. Yolanda leaned over the sink.

'Sorry. Did it hurt? Are you okay?'

Yolanda was spitting, tongue-tied, not looking at me. I gave her the rest of my flask instead of saying sorry again.

§

That was a monster out there. Two a.m., the second week. I smelled her through the vents. Wine teeth, beef stock, salivation. My mother still would not turn on the air conditioning. My father had changed to night shift at the hospital. He said at home it was too goddamned hot.

Barbra peeked through the crack of my door. 'I'll just sit at the bed, okay, until you fall asleep.'

She wore green satin short shorts and a tight white tank top with cartoon-looking lace. She had worn this during the day.

I felt guilty about what had happened between us. I'd left some books for her to borrow on the basement stairs, Arthur Koestler and Colette. I didn't think she'd read those books in Israel. Barbra had been taking Abigail to camp every day and Abigail told me that people there thought Barbra was her *nanny*. I thought that was totally fucked up. Don't people know that an almost-twelve-year-old girl doesn't need a fucking nanny?

I'd avoided Barbra successfully all week. Pretty much every day I went to the tennis club with Joel, who kept asking me if Barbra was as hot as she looked in her picture or what. I hated his tennis. I hated every sport.

'Maybe he's interested in tennis lessons?' my father said to my mother. 'You know, maybe he'll get off his ass?'

'Maybe you should ask him,' my mother said.

Joel even thought I liked watching his athletics. He bragged about going to some summer championship thing. I watched him scuttle around the court like a bisected ant. The ball made a sound as stupid as him. *Guh*, each time he hit the thing. I imagined a poisonous spray can, chasing him. Tennis was ping-fucking-pong. I thought that at the end of *Letter to the Father*, Kafka would finally speak truth to his dad.

'You see me beat that little shit into the turf?' Joel always said after practice.

Joel wanted to meet Barbra. He said I should bring her to one of his games.

Tonight, in my room, Barbra seemed only tipsy, not drunk. Her tank top looked like lingerie. Since she'd come to my room that first time, I was terrified that she thought I was racist. I could not stop thinking about it. Like, *did* I only like her because of the colour of her skin? Because of the pine-needle hairs peeking out from her armpits? Because of the roll in her belly, her beef-stock bubble sweat, loam under our house – God, the walls were buckling from her heat. She was here again, back again, at the foot of my bed.

'Why are you so scared of me, bruh?'

Ever since I was fourteen, my mother stored a box of condoms in the basement. I could not remember: did *someone* in Israel treat her like a dog? Or did she say dogs? Was it multiple people, multiple dogs?

'I asked you, why are you so scared of me now?'

I'd scratched my scrawny white thighs when I'd jerked off not thinking of her.

'Are all you Jew-boys in Canada so scared?'

'What'd you just say?'

Jew-boy was anti-Semitic.

'You fucking trembling now or what?'

Did they have gang-bangers in Israel? Why was she talking to me like that and laughing? Israel had fucking *rescued* her!

'Maybe you should leave now,' I croaked. I wrung my sweaty hands together.

'Trembling, look. He's *trembling!*'

I wanted her out of my room, her roiling open-mouthed glee. It occurred to me right then that *she* was the racist. *She* was anti-Semitic. She was a person on purpose swinging me round! I banged left and banged right, my head hit the ceiling. How could a Jewish girl who was rescued by a Jewish country actually *hate* that country? I wanted to know: did she hate us or Israel? And what the fuck was *Jew-boy*? Was *Jew-boy* code for *white boy*? Joel said that when he turned eighteen he was going on Birthright. 'For the bitches,' he said. 'Girls are hotter with guns.'

God, I felt afflicted by a nightmare in my real life.

Barbra stayed on my bed, sparkling in her green satin shorts.

'Your dad says he wants me to go to university here.'

I held my leg. It was bouncing. No, my father didn't say that. He said *program*. I didn't want to tell her, he meant *community college*. 'And,' my father said, 'they had to fundraise, talk to Bill, do the corn roast and school talks and church talks, get a lawyer, a lawyer who specialized in these things.'

She flopped on my bed sideways, landing perfect. I was junk.

'Barbra will decide,' my mom said. 'She can do anything she wants to.'

'If you think getting a foreign student the right visa is so easy, *you try and do it*,' my father said.

My mother looked at me, rolling her eyes. I know both me and my mother thought that my father thought that Barbra should study cooking or nursing. Both me and my mother thought my father was being a dick.

'What do you two smartasses know about immigration?' my father challenged.

'I know that a foreign student can't get into university without the right credits,' my mother said. '*I* had to go back and do high school science to get into social work, remember? And I'm a card-carrying, full-blooded Canadian!'

Something about Barbra in our house made my mother almost giddy, as if all her anger was liquefying into glee.

My father turned to me, agitated. 'And what do *you* know, smart guy?'

I knew that my father hadn't read a book basically since high school.

Barbra shifted onto her back. 'I *do* want to go to university,' she said. 'But I don't need any of you people to help me get in.'

I checked to make sure my bedroom door was really shut. She could not read my mind. I thought maybe *Jew-boy* was a test.

'Uh, yeah, my dad's just trying to do the technical stuff,' I said. 'But I think you can just write an essay or something to apply. Then, like, you don't need to do all those Rotary talks or whatever…'

Barbra shot me a look. 'You think I'm dumb?'

'*No!*'

My *no* was way too insistent.

'You think I *wanted* to come here?'

'I don't know,' I said quickly, wishing I'd said nothing at all.

'My uncle told me this was one last thing they could try before they set me on the streets.'

My hands kept sweating. The *streets*? Who was her uncle? Kids who have uncles are orphans? Was she not a real orphan?

'Anyway, I don't care if he thinks it's punishment being here. Punishment, banishment. Same thing. I'm an expert.'

'An expert at what?'

The air in my room hung hot between us.

Barbra stared at the ceiling. She put both her hands near the elastic rim of her shorts. 'Getting a new family,' she said. 'A new family. A new country. A brand new fuckin' name.'

Then Barbra got up on one elbow and stared at me with this little open-mouthed grin. I returned it. Exhaled. I had more questions. Like, structural questions. My dad said her family *gave her up*. He said she'd been without her family for *years*.

'So, uh, who is this dude? I mean, your "uncle"?'

Was her uncle the literal, fucking dog?

Barbra started to laugh. 'Uh, my father's *brother*? That's an uncle, right? He's lived in Israel since '84. My parents wanted me to get a real education. I hate the guy. I can't do anything with him. And my aunt is his baby machine. Five kids when I got there. They had no room for me.'

'But why didn't your parents ever come to Israel?'

'Look, I don't know, bruh,' Barbra said.

She turned away from me and lay on her side on my bed. Soon she started stroking her own waist. I just watched her, feeling my cock pulse on repeat. 'You believe that I've read all your fucking books?'

'Yes,' I said quickly, thinking about the fact that her coming here was punishment. I kept blinking. For what? She was being punished for *what*?

Barbra started laughing. 'You're funny,' she said, rolling on to her back.

Maybe this trip, maybe staying with our family, was all just one big joke to her?

Suddenly, Barbra pulled up her T-shirt.

I got this cracking ice feeling inside my rib cage.

She was staring at me. I looked at her tits. They were oblong and swollen, with diamond-shaped eyes.

'Jew-boy, come on. Stop being so scared.'

She rolled side to side so her tits jiggled a little. I had lock-jaw. *Jew-boy.*

'I know Kafka. Relax. I like *Amerika*.'

Barbra pushed her tits together. My head got increasingly heavy. It felt like she was thriving while I was lodged in the ice.

'Kafka was a migrant. He knew about us.'

My forehead bobbed lower. Barbra read Kafka. Kafka was not a migrant. Who did she mean, *us*?

'Come here,' Barbra said.

I remembered the Queen of Sheba from Hebrew school. The Queen of Sheba was from Ethiopia. Barbra left Addis Ababa when she was five.

I felt my mouth dry, sort of snapping like a turtle's. I felt myself pitching forward at the waist.

'Closer,' she said.

My mouth found one nipple, a marble. It filled my whole mouth, iridescent, swelling. Operation Solomon meant immigration. My forehead kept butting into her chest. I tasted sugar in the marble, iridescent juice. I had to read *Amerika* now. My mouth kept slipping off her nipple because she kept jiggling. Was she still laughing at me? I pushed her tits together. What was her real name? I got all the fat. I wanted both in my mouth. Was I racist? I gathered up the sides of her breasts.

'Operation Solomon was a *miracle*,' my father said.

Barbra held on to a lock of my hair at the forehead. She tried to move me like that, back and forth. It was like she was holding a leash, like my head was the dog.

In Israel, she'd said, they treat us like dogs.

Rabid, I clamped down. I slathered and sucked both her tits.

I remembered that the Queen of Sheba tried to trick the king, but King Solomon was smarter – he answered every one of her riddles. The king *knew* about women, my Hebrew teacher said.

Barbra bucked. My bed creaked. It was like we were fighting. I was on top of her, sweating, suctioned like a bat. Barbra started moaning. I kept kneading her fat, almost biting her nipples. I was good at this. My father gushed about Operation Solomon. He kept saying to Barbra it was a revelation for him. 'If a modern-day country could manufacture a modern-day Exodus, if a modern-day country could solve a humanitarian crisis, save thousands and thousands, *fourteen thousand* Jews from a *famine*, well, that was really something, wasn't it? The Jews did this, heroic, in forty-eight hours!' My father's voice cracked. *Hallelujah*, I said. What the fuck was Barbra supposed to say? *Thank you, Father? Thank you, Uncle? Thank you for saving me?* Good tits stuck in blouses. Hard purple nipples with juice. Barbra the orphan said nothing. No gushing. Not grateful. I sucked her the hardest. I kept making her moan. I pinned her arms down so that she could just take it, so that *she* was the one who was trembling now. She was burning up. I felt her hand creep to her shorts. I kept on sucking, tongue wagging. I wanted to yank the elastic. I wanted to grab her hot hand and replace it with mine. My father made Israel sound totally righteous. My father thought he was eliminating pain. The smell from her shorts was like milk on the verge. Her nipples touched the dome of my mouth.

'You're good at this,' she moaned. 'You make me feel good.'

The saviour fantasy was not eliminating pain.

My father never asked Barbra questions. Like, how on earth do you feel? *You feel good. You feel good.* How did you feel when you left your real home? My hand got raked over her heap of red coals. *This is good. This is good.* I wanted to slide my finger inside her.

The Queen of Sheba had sex with King Solomon. Joel said it was the first interracial love affair. Barbra, how did it feel to be lifted by soldiers? How did it feel to be sent to your uncle? Everyone in our Hebrew class laughed. I scratched her pubic hairs. Interracial. Barbra bucked. I kept sucking. I touched underneath her sheepskin lips. I felt sprouting. A suction. I put my fingertip down. No breathing. I slid in. The space fit my finger. I did a little C-stroke. I heard myself moaning. *You feel good. You feel good.* My knuckle got gripped. I used my second hand, too. One finger inside and one C-stroking thumb. Mushy, sinuous. A little bump. I was inside her. Perched over her. I never wanted it to change.

All of a sudden, her hand pushed my hands away.

'What?' I said. '*What?*'

It felt like a plug being pulled. I sat up and stared at one shiny spot on her shorts. I wiped my hands on the sheets. I felt weird, she looked weird. Barbra half-sat back up.

'They told me these Canadians were gonna be very naive.'

I still felt her nipples like lozenges, numb in my mouth.

'You people think you can do *anything.*'

'No…'

'Think about it, Jew-boy.'

'Think about *what?*'

I looked down at myself. My cock stuck still in my jeans, starfish wrinkles at my crotch.

I wanted to drop to my knees and just beg her, say: *Jew-boy wants back in to your patch!*

But Barbra got up off my bed. I knew that *you people* meant me and my dad. She staggered out of my room, without looking back. I felt cold. I wanted to fuck her. I wanted to be with her, know her real name. God, I felt guilty. I really didn't understand why she'd left me right then.

I went to the site that Joel showed me of girls with no makeup with cum on their faces. They looked like Renaissance chicks with post-fuck pink cheeks, with their pulled-back hair and tilted heads. I wanted Barbra's face. I wanted her face back in front of me. I wanted to drown her forehead in cum. I wanted to see my cum roll down her cheeks, stream over on her lips. I rubbed myself hard. *Amerika.* I imagined her still here, right between my legs. I wanted to make her lick me and taste it. I wanted to know what she thought about me. I wanted to lie here all night and read with her, finger her, do what she wanted. I imaged my cock right in front of her face. Divining rod. Spraying this whole airless place.

By the time the sun rose, I'd sprayed her five times.

I thought, I'll let her call me Jew-boy for life.

§

My mother used to say that no one under thirty should have to take care of a kid. My mother said that when she got pregnant with me, my father promised he would split the work of baby care with her. She said they made a bargain that they would do things equally, that she would take time off teaching high school and he would pull back on his hours at the hospital – 'all of it a bargain he *did not keep*,' my mother said. She told me that my father wouldn't get up in the middle of the night to give me a bottle. She said he was furious the first time that she woke him up to do it. 'You were screaming,' my mother told me, 'like how babies scream, and your father started cursing at me – this is the middle of the night – and he's yelling, goddamn it, *someone* in this goddamned house has to work, Ruth!' My mother always imitated my father's voice when she talked about him. She always said her own name with this particular spite. 'Your father actually called me a *bitch* for waking him up – *bitch* is so nice to hear with a newborn shrieking, of course – and when I told him I absolutely would not stand for *that word,* he said he did not remember it, he said he would *never* call me such a bad name. He said, maybe it was in his sleep. He feigned innocence.'

'I clocked that one,' my mother said. And even though it never happened again, my mother told me that when she was on maternity leave, she was pissed off at my father the whole time she was pushing me around the city in a stroller. Then she said her doctor told her that her eggs would dry up if she didn't get pregnant again soon. She was thirty-three years old. And then she had a miscarriage. My mother said it was awful and really, really painful. She said there was blood all over the bathroom floor and she could barely get up and she called my dad at work and he said he couldn't leave so she called his mother. 'Your Bubie Marsha had to come to our house to help me clean it all up. Your Bubie Marsha,' my mother told me, 'did that for your dad.' I felt weird when she told me all this. Like I felt guilty, almost guilty by proxy for my father. Or it was too much information. Miscarriage blood. But my mother didn't get it. She said she liked telling me things that happened when I was a kid. But to me it felt like a kind of transplanted revenge against my father. That miscarriage, as my mother told it, made her realize that she actually *wanted* to have another a baby. And my dad agreed with her that I shouldn't be an only child, that siblings were good. And so my mother got pregnant with Abigail almost five years after me and she said that after Abigail she sort of fell into a rhythm, as if she finally accepted my dad's essential breadwinner position and that her taking over with us kids was necessary, i.e., for the greater good.

'Yeah, it was for society,' my mother said, laughing. '*Some-one* has to privilege the fucking family.'

My mother said that she didn't ever regret being a full-time, stay-at-home mom for so long – 'because look at you and Abigail. My children are amazing. Everyone I know says that to me.'

I didn't feel amazing. I felt totally average. And Abigail was amazing, but, come on, not in the typical sense.

It was my mother, in fact, who was amazing. My mother bought me condoms. Joel said that was fucked. But I know my mother was just trying to prepare me for sex.

Nuria was fifteen. We were both fifteen. I remember the night that I took her out for pizza and burned the roof of my mouth on the cheese. We came home around ten o'clock and went down to the basement. It seemed like both my parents were asleep. Actually, my mother told me that she'd told my father to knock on the door if I was ever in the basement with Nuria, so I knew that we were safe. I imagined doing it with her on the couch in front of the TV. Nuria, though, wanted to actually watch TV – some hospital drama – and I was kind of surprised. I tried to put my hand down her pants. She was fleshy. I liked that. My hand got stuck. I had to unzip her jeans first. She panted at the TV as if she were scared. Nuria had shaved. It was weird. I didn't recognize her vagina.

Joel said, 'Sluts shave so you can lick without choking.'

'Do you like it?' Nuria asked, staring at the TV.

'Yeah, sort of,' I said, not wanting to hurt her feelings. I got on my knees in front of her. I guess it was okay that she was watching TV. I had a condom in my pocket. I pulled her pants off all the way. I stared at her shaved vagina. I seriously did not recognize it. I mean, I'd seen vaginas like this before from Joel and his porn, but it reminded me of my sister, I mean, being a kid and being naked. It made me feel woozy.

I'd been hard and then I lost it. I saw a bright red pimple on Nuria's thigh. I pretended to look for the condom. I told Nuria to stay where she was, that I just had to go to the bathroom. I didn't even feel like having sex anymore. But when I returned, Nuria was lying sideways on the couch and all her clothes were off. She was pretending she was sleeping. She didn't even open her eyes when I crouched over her, saying her name. She giggled. When she giggled like that, I got hard. I ripped open the condom. I took a while to put it on even though I'd practised. I pinched the head of the thing. It felt too slippery. It went on right the second time. All I felt was the tight roll of the condom, the cement smell of the basement walls. Nuria kept giggling. She was wet when I went in. It was not what I thought it would feel like. She squealed. It felt too plastic or squishy. I was disappointed. This was it. I felt my ass clench. That felt good. It felt like the room shrunk. I just wanted to stay inside of myself inside of her. Then Nuria, at some point, punched up on my chest.

'What?' I groaned. 'Stop hitting me.'

When a man hits a woman he lives with, said my mother, it's called *domestic abuse*.

'Stop!' Nuria said, bouncing around on the couch.

I sluiced out of her body like a zipper going down. Immediately, I came inside the whole condom. I was off balance. My feet were sweating. I tried to kiss her face, then her tits. Nuria was acting so weird, trying to swim away from me. It was as if I'd done something wrong, something on purpose. She really didn't want me to kiss her, she wanted to get up. So I stopped.

Doctors and nurses worked on the TV. My condom was the colour of turnip. It was only eleven o'clock. Nuria put on her clothes and was calling her brother to come pick her up.

'Why are you so mad?' I remember I kept saying. I could tell Nuria was trying not to cry. I didn't want her to leave. Soon, we heard Nuria's brother outside. I thought, the horn of abuse. I never had sex with Nuria again.

§

My father had not gotten used to the fact almost three weeks in that I wasn't going to get a summer job. Since Barbra had arrived, he'd said at least once a day: 'I don't know of a job where a kid just sits on his trap hole and reads.'

'My butt's not a trap hole,' I answered.

'Right. The trap hole's your mouth.'

'Nope. The trap hole is actually the crack in the system.'

'Jesus Christ,' my father sighed. 'Semantics and hijinks aren't going to get you into law school – you know that, right? One day you're going to have to learn to be employable just like the rest of us.'

I laughed. My father thought I wanted to be a nutbag surgeon like him? I wasn't going to take Barbra to the fucking CN Tower, like he suggested. And I wasn't going to drag her through bird shit in High Park like my mother thought I should. All I wanted was to stay in our house. Wait for night. I wanted to psychically lure her back up to my room and beg like a Jew-boy to start all over again.

Can I show you where I get Kafka? I sent my über-polite text down to her in the basement.

After a few minutes Barbra texted back *yes*.

I sent her the address of Abacus and a link to a story I'd just read about Kafka's tuberculosis.

The next day I waited for Barbra outside the bookstore at

noon. She was late. I kept checking my phone. I knew she'd dropped off Abigail a few hours ago. I thought maybe I shouldn't have sent her that tuberculosis story. I should've sent her something more sexy, relevant.

Finally, in the warping hot sun, I saw her walking toward me, teetering a little. She definitely was not walking in a straight line. But she arrived right at the same time as Jim the owner and his dog.

'Uh, this is Barbra, our exchange student,' I said to Jim, clearing my throat, trying to do the right kind of introduction.

'I went to the wrong park this morning,' Jim said, nodding at Barbra. 'Apparently, no dogs allowed. The parents got security cameras. This is the town we're living in now.'

Jim opened the door for us. The bookshelves floor to ceiling all seemed to cave inward. I wanted to explain the layout to Barbra, but she just wandered away while Jim kept on talking about canine surveillance.

After a few minutes, I excused myself from Jim. I wondered if he could tell what was going on between us. I'd spent hours and hours with Jim talking about Kafka.

I found Barbra in US History. 'My mom gave me her credit card. She said to buy you anything you wanted.'

Barbra shrugged. Her breath smelled like wine.

'I'll be in European Literature,' I told her. Since when had she been drinking? 'You want to come? See the Kafka?'

'Nah, bruh, I'm good,' Barbra said.

I left her, eyes pink, holding on to the bookshelf. Jim played some kind of talk radio station. I wanted to tell the whole world that I'd sucked on her tits. My mother's credit card was my father's credit card. Did she drink this much in Israel? Was *that* why her uncle had sent her away?

I touched the spine of *The Last Temptation of Christ*. For some reason that book always appeared – like, not just at Jim's – no matter what bookstore I was in. Day-drinking, I knew, signified a problem. Jim didn't have *Amerika*. I shuffled back to the Civil War stacks. Barbra wasn't there. I went around the corner to Black Studies, then to Feminism.

'She went down to the basement,' Jim called out.

My shoelace caught on a splinter in the floorboard. The staircase down was too narrow. Open walls with pink fibreglass. The basement had a hanging trampoline ceiling. It was even more labyrinthine than upstairs and smelled like the glue of papier mâché.

I found Barbra in the Jewish Studies section, squatting at the shelf closest to the floor. All the books on the top shelves in this section were encyclopedia sets with embossed gold Hebrew letters, touching each other by threads.

'What are you finding down *here*?' my voice boomed.

God, if my father wasn't present, why did I have to sound like him?

Barbra had a big stack of books between her sandals. I saw each one of her moon-coloured toenails.

She passed me up a book that weighed at least five pounds. 'Heard about him?'

'I hated Hebrew school. I know *nothing* down here.'

Barbra ignored me. The book had an etched drawing on the cover of a morose-looking, bearded, bonnet-headed man: *Sabbatai Zevi: The Mystical Messiah*.

'I don't think you're going to be able to read this all in a month,' I said, pretending to weight-lift with the thing.

Barbra stood up. Her knees cracked. She was wearing a tight linen dress. She headed upstairs, careening, and plunged her hand into exposed fibreglass. I followed the back of her, reading the thousand-page thing:

> *The only messianic movement to engulf the whole of Jewry –*
> *from England to Persia, from Germany to Morocco, from Poland*
> *to Yemen – was that aroused by a young kabbalist rabbi from*
> *Smyrna, the 'messiah' Sabbatai Zevi and his prophet, Nathan*
> *of Gaza, in 1666.*

I remembered it was Joel who told me that Jesus was Jewish. I didn't believe him, at first. Why would Jesus be Jewish? That had seemed totally ludicrous to me. And Nathan of Gaza – uh, I didn't think someone named Nathan would be wandering around Gaza. I wanted to tell Barbra all of my jokes. 1666: the year Jewry – *Jewry?* – was undone!

At the front desk, Jim told Barbra that this book was one of a kind. Then he asked her what she knew about the Zohar.

'*Book of the Hidden* influenced every single stage of Sabbatai's journey,' Jim said, 'so you might be kind of lost if you just start with this.'

'I am not starting anything,' Barbra said.

Jim looked at me over his glasses, surprised.

'Barbra's from Israel,' I said quickly, handing Jim my mother's credit card. 'She probably learned about this stuff in, like, high school – am I right?'

Barbra stared out the greasy glass door of the bookstore. 'Yeah. What we learn in this life, the DNA already knows.'

She walked away from us, holding her arms slightly out. I felt embarrassed. I knew Jim wasn't trying to challenge Barbra. I knew Jim just loved talking books and making links. I took Barbra's book from him in a paper bag. Why'd she choose this? This was not literature. Was she trying to impress my father?

'What are you going to do now?' I asked her outside on the street.

'Read,' Barbra said, rolling her eyes at me.

I handed her the book. We walked for a few blocks in silence. I didn't know what to say because I felt like anything I said then would be wrong. But I wanted to ask her what she was talking about in the store. Did she mean that we're born with what we know and that's it? Was she implying she had a God-given superiority?

Barbra popped gum that smelled sickeningly cherry. I felt it spray down on my head.

§

Joel told me they'd nicknamed Barbra 'the giraffe.' He wanted his asshole friends from the tennis club to meet her. But it was starting to be impossible to get Barbra to go out. She'd told my mother that she didn't want to pick up Abigail. She told my father she didn't want to have dinners with us either. I think the first few nights of her missing were okay, it almost felt like things were back to some kind of normal for my family. But after four nights in a row, I think we all started feeling the same. Rejected, desperate. Abigail said she felt depressed. Every dinner she whined, 'What is Barbra *doing* down there?'

It was the end of the third week of July. I knew what Barbra was doing. I didn't tell my parents. Reading and drinking until she passed out. I felt like it was a secret – just like my awareness that *Barbra* was not her real name. If I kept her secrets, I thought, I'd get her back to my bed.

I'd learned from the internet that Sabbatai Zevi was from Smyrna, born in 1626. Back then, every Jewish boy studied the

Torah all day, instead of going to a regular school. I read that he rebelled as a teenager; he started to display so-called strange behaviour, like kissing the Torah and eating forbidden foods. By the time he was eighteen years old, Sabbatai Zevi was excommunicated from Smyrna. He wandered around Turkey and Italy, got married twice, had both marriages annulled, and then, I don't know when – Wikipedia didn't tell me – the mofo began to think of himself as the Messiah. He was wandering around Europe preaching about women and their freedom – a far cry from *cheder* – and somehow he ended up in Egypt, where he met this guy Nathan, a visionary kid from Jerusalem. Anyway, Nathan and Sabbatai really hit it off. They decided to preach more strange behaviour and keep titillating the ladies. By the time Nathan moved to Gaza to continue his studies and help spread Sabbatai's liberation message, Sabbatai married his third wife, Sarah, a Polish orphan who'd worked as a prostitute.

Another Jewish Jesus, I deduced, mad into bromance and whores!

I couldn't wait to talk to Barbra about this.

But, truly, she would not come up from the basement.

My mother kept asking me if I knew what the hell was going on. She said, 'The girl's eating baked beans straight out of the can down there.'

My father said he cancelled two Rotary fundraising talks because Barbra told him she wasn't feeling well.

I thought, botulism and self-sequestering: it's *messianic*.

I knew it was kind of my secret job to get her out of this funk. I wanted to creep down and ask her these pertinent questions: What do you like about that rabbi motherfucker? What do you want from your last month in our house? Do you really want a visa? You really want to go to school here?

I'll get you a bottle. Five bottles. What's your real name? Can we fuck? Can we fuck? Tell me your innermost thoughts, then we fuck? I'll get you your visa. And then we fuck.

My mental incursions were useless. Barbra would not come up.

But on August first, she sent me a text at four a.m.: *Do you believe in a punishing God?*

I held my phone. Trembling. Now I was really trembling. I saw my sticky white hands scratching her violin back.

I do not believe in a punishing God, I wrote back. *I do not believe in a banishing God.*

Punishment, banishment. She was not the expert.

Calmly, righteously, I send this last thought: *I believe in drugs. Joel has all the drugs.*

Mom and Dad, you should thank me. I smoked Barbra out of her hole.

§

I sat on one side of Barbra in the theatre and Joel sat on the other. She was so skinny from not eating that I saw a pulse near her breastbone. Anton and Brandon were on the other side of Joel. Joel said it wasn't every day that two private-school fuckers meet a hot Black chick from Israel.

Fuck off, you racists, I wanted to say.

But Barbra, I didn't get it, just started laughing.

Joel showed her his flask in the semi-dark. 'My dad's rum is sick. It's from Jam-rock. You want some in your coke?'

'Yah, mon, I'm a rum head,' Barbra replied.

Joel looked at me, fuck yes-ing, sticking two fingers up between his bangs. Why was she play-acting like this with him?

Joel plopped two hits of rum into Barbra's cup. I'd had to bribe her out of the basement but now she seemed so comfortable or something. Anton and Brandon were laughing as the movie began. What exactly had changed? My mother was worried. My father distanced himself. Why was she now just drinking and joking with these UCC fuckers as if nothing were wrong? I thought I'd known what was wrong. Anton and Brandon had their own flask. God, I hated Joel. I hated that Joel was showing off my girlfriend by proxy.

The opening of V for Vendetta was high-pitched and bombastic.

Was Barbra my girlfriend? I wanted her to be. I knew I'd do anything for this to be.

'Do you believe God punishes people?'

It occurred to me that I'd never asked Barbra back the question. It occurred to me that I needed possession of her right now. Barbra looked at me sideways in silence, eyes weirdly animated from the actors onscreen.

'You know I do,' Barbra whispered back to me.

According to Jewishmysticism.com, Sabbatai Zevi's wife, Sarah, was raised in Poland by nuns because when she was a baby her family had been killed in the Chmielnicki massacres. Allegedly, as a teenager, she wandered around Europe pretending she was Christian, having sex to survive. Later, Sarah said that she always knew she was meant to marry the Messiah.

Joel took the lid off of Barbra's extra-size Coke and topped her up with his mickey of rum. Joel acted like an ass with his friends. Their plan was to get loaded in the middle of the day.

Barbra sucked through her straw. 'God is backwards, upside-down.'

Was this something that that messianic mofo liked to say?

Barbra had promised to do a Rotary event with my father that evening. It was a city-wide meet-and-greet for all the summer scholarship students. Barbra was wearing this spandex tank-top dress that pushed her tits out and showed her small rolls of waist flesh. I wanted to crash the event, cheering for her, if she wore this same dress and her leather sandal with the laces criss-crossed up to her calves.

As we watched the film, I kept glancing at Joel's hand. It seemed bent like a claw, appearing in fog. It slow-drummed the armrest between him and her. I watched him in my peripheral vision. I kept my vision split between the screen and his fingers. *V for Vendetta* had too many cuts. The claw put itself on her naked forearm. I read that Alan Moore didn't even want his name on the film. Joel's hand shone in the darkness. I smelled rum on her breath. Natalie Portman was about to get her head shaved. Barbra suddenly slung her arm around the back of my chair. Her armpit had all those pine-needle hairs. I got a blast of her sweat, her germination. Natalie Portman had a strangely small head. I knew already Joel thought Barbra was hot. I saw movement in the sand, the hand on the thigh. Unbelievable, fuck. She was totally out of his league. Joel had no idea she actually thought he was racist. Anton and Brandon were racists! I nuzzled my snout in her armpit. I hadn't told Joel what was happening with us. I would never tell Joel what was happening with us. I had the bucket of popcorn between my sweatpants. Natalie Portman's face shook when she screamed. I licked Barbra's armpit. Joel lifted her spandex. Natalie Portman was fragile. Barbra was *mine*. My tongue stuck on the needles. Natalie Portman spoke Hebrew. I imagined a rabbinic, narcissistic, messianic manic-depressive taking over Barbra's mind. Natalie Portman loomed above us. She was being deloused, giant-sized. I sluiced my tongue around in circles inside Barbra's pit. Joel's hand disappeared. Barbra used her thighs to push him away. Onscreen, Natalie Portman trembled and cried.

Joel whispered to Barbra: 'She looks like a Suicide Girl.'

My face stayed stuck in her cobweb of sweat. Barbra, I thought, had been punished *unfairly*. Not by God – by her uncle, by life.

'What's a Suicide Girl?' Barbra asked.

I heard Joel on the other side of her spandex. 'It's porno for girls with rings through their clits.'

Barbra hiccupped then burped. She pushed me away.

The pelt of Natalie Portman slithered off to each side.

'Why *suicide*?' Barbra whispered. 'What does that name mean?'

Someone lobbed a handful of popcorn at us from behind.

Natalie Portman was going ballistic. I thought, that girl is thinking about the Holocaust.

Barbra took the lid off her drink and guzzled the dregs. Joel poured her another hit of rum. He scrolled through his phone. I took Barbra's hand. It was burning up.

'Are you okay?' I whispered.

It felt like a force field of fire suddenly encased her. Joel showed us a picture on his phone all aglow: a green-haired girl on her bony white knees, wrists crossed, sleeves tattooed with skulls and barbed wire.

'This one's got a double barbell in her hood and a stud in her clit.'

I heard Joel's saliva. I did not want to be here. Suddenly, Barbra pushed up from her seat. I watched her disappear into the darkness. Joel laughed at my face. Skull's eyes and barbed wire.

'Fuck you, bro,' I said.

I went out to the lobby just a few seconds behind Barbra, but she wasn't anywhere there. I paced in front of the women's bathroom. I heard Natalie Portman whining from inside. I was licking my lips. I felt totally stressed. I felt like I had to possess her to keep her revelations all mine. A ticket guy in a suit started walking over toward me. I inched away from the women's bathroom door. I kind of knew I was catastrophizing – that is what my mother would've said. Like, there was no actual reason for me to link up suicide and Barbra. Or suicide and porn, suicide and being punished. Would she ever tell me about the dogs of Israel? Or was I just like Joel? Pink, pimply, porn-peddling? My thinking felt skewed. Why did she let him put his paw on her? My mother studied catastrophes for women. My mother was always right.

Maybe God had had enough of Barbra. Maybe God would punish *me* now.

Barbra waltzed out of the washroom.

'Are you okay?' I said, racing. 'I thought something was wrong.'

She walked right past me. 'You thought wrong, Jew-boy.'

I lost my breath. My chest liquefied. All I could do was trot back into the theatre behind her.

§

Me and my mother waited up for Barbra and my father that night in the kitchen, drinking coffee. He hadn't wanted either of us to come to the Rotary event.

He said, 'Barbra needs to concentrate on meeting the other students. We have a few from Guatemala and we've got this sharp eighteen-year-old pre-med girl from Peru.'

But when they arrived back home that night after eleven o'clock, Barbra's eyes were bright pink. Her face seemed so wild. I remembered her gulping consumption of Joel's Jam-rock rum. Barbra immediately shot down to the basement and I stood up to follow but my mother shushed quietly at me, 'Let her be, let her be.'

Me and my mother had been mid-conversation. My mother told me she was worried about me. My mother asked me if I needed some mental support. 'Sixteen,' she said, 'is a vulnerable time for a guy.' My mother looked at me as if she was searching for clues. I was not sure what clues or what *vulnerable* meant. Then my mother told me that she'd gotten a teaching job out of town. She said she'd miss my birthday in September but that I could visit. What I wanted to tell her was what I thought was going on with Barbra when Barbra and my father came in.

'There's coffee,' my mother said wearily, after Barbra ran downstairs. 'What's wrong now? What happened? What did you do?'

My father ignored my mother and went to pour himself a cup. Coffee did not keep any of us from sleeping.

'She called herself an "exile,"' my father said, bewildered. 'I don't think she knows the right word. That is not the right word.'

My heart pounded. *Exile* was a Sabbatai Zevi thing.

My father said Barbra seemed out of it at the meeting. 'She got too skinny, Ruth. What's her problem? We can't send her back like that.'

'Just tell us what happened,' I said, without freaking out at my father that he said we were sending her back.

'What's with *you* now?' My dad shot me a look.

I looked at the floor. I felt like he could read my fucking mind. Skulls and barbed wire. The end of exile.

My father slurped from his mug. 'So, she started talking at the church, we had at least fifty guys there, and it was okay, she started just fine, but then she's talking about Operation Solomon, which is *fine*, that's all good, but then she's telling this story about how she didn't want to go, she loved her country, she meant Ethiopia, okay, and she says that some young soldier in a helmet just picks her up out of the crowd and, uh, is holding her tightly, and feeling under her little dress or whatever she's wearing, and I'm telling you, okay, look, all this was pretty abrupt.'

I could not control my labouring breath. She was *abused*. That's what she meant when she said *they treat us like dogs*.

I knew that my father was unconscious of the drama that was playing out between us.

'Then she said, and I quote: "The Jew put me inside a military plane."'

My father coughed. He took a few more gulps of coffee.

'All of us were on our knees in the pews,' my father said. 'And I know Bob and the others did not appreciate or understand that picture of, you know, her skirt, the military, a child being, I don't know, grabbed? It could not have been on purpose. This did not happen on purpose. And why use that word in particular? *Jew*. Yes, okay, we all know Israel has a military…'

'It sounds like she was just speaking her truth,' my mother finally interrupted. 'I don't think this is about the discomfort of Bob or whoever.'

'Yeah, I *know* that, Ruth. I know that, but you weren't there. It was a little embarrassing for the other kids in the program, too.'

Before my mother and father could get into some kind of fresh melee, I asked: 'Was she crying?'

My mother looked at me and smiled. Maybe feeling vulnerable was good.

'She was talking about some sticker on her forehead,' my father continued. 'Some number on her forehead that was put on the sticker and she said she didn't remember the number… She seemed uncomfortable, we were uncomfortable, that's all I knew. And then she told us that they measured her forehead and took her fingerprints and gave her drugs. This was in *Israel*, not Ethiopia. She started talking about some "holding camp." That's what she called it. She said they measured her head in a holding camp. Ruth, I'm telling you, she made it sound like some kind of program of eugenics. And this was supposed to be a good evening for us, good for fundraising, light stuff, and she made it look bad on us, okay? It looks really, really bad.'

The line between my mother's eyes was as straight as a ruler.

'She was making the Jews look like monsters, okay?'

'I think you mean Nazis,' my mother said.

My father cursed. 'Jesus. That's cheap.'

The melee between them could not be prevented. I thought about Barbra's head measured and taped.

'What that girl said was a *lie*, Ruth. She said she arrived in Israel "all alone." She said she was in a "camp," okay, for six weeks."

I imagined Bob Cunningham and my father rushing the stage, my father gripping Barbra's elbow and Barbra letting herself be passed off to Bob in the wings. I imagined my father heading back out to explain to the men and all the other exchange students that Operation Solomon was a *miracle*! Israel rescued fourteen thousand persecuted, starving Jews in under two days!

'Barbra obviously carries trauma about this,' my mother said.

'But there were no "holding camps" in Israel, Ruth! Maybe the Ethiopians were held somewhere for a day after landing – a few days, tops.'

I believed the term: *holding camps.* I believed term *exile,* too.

'Barbra clearly identifies as an oppressed young woman,' my mother said slowly, standing up. 'And this is a form of self-empowerment for her. You and Bob and, look, the whole Rotary Club, you *have* to accept this. You cannot bring kids here and – what? – not accept they might have some psychological needs? Not every girl is a pre-med, okay? Why can't she tell you she's conflicted? Why can't you see that she's in pain?'

'Shhh, Ruth, stop it. It's not that,' my father hissed. I know he was afraid of Barbra hearing him call her a liar. 'That girl has had *every* advantage after being rescued from poverty and a country that did not want her. She *grew up* in Israel. She was rescued when she was *five.*'

'Coming to Israel at five does not mean blank slate.'

'But saying she was alone for six weeks in a *camp*? A) That's a lie, Ruth, and B) provocative! Is she suggesting that Israel did something *wrong*? I mean, that is crazy! It's just crazy! It's backwards. Upside down.'

Upside down. Backwards. I started to falter.

'The Rotarians evidently need some trauma education,' my mother said. 'There is a tendency – and this has been *proven* – for relocated kids to dissociate.'

'*Relocate*? *Dissociate*? Ruth, it's called making *aliyah*!'

My mother yawned. 'I think we should all have some empathy for that scared little girl who was taken from her home and very likely abused.'

'Abused? She was given a *home*. She was adopted, for Christ's sake. She was taken *care* of by Jews! She is a Jew! The Rotarians understand – they know about Operation Solomon. And they believe that Israel has a right to exist! Everything, my God, is not about trauma and abuse!'

My father stormed out of the room with his coffee. My mother looked at me, eyes dancing. 'Your father can only spout so much bullshit,' she said, 'because for some reason he thinks he's never done anything bad.'

Bad. And God is backwards.

Yeah, I knew *exactly* why Barbra had called herself an exile. I knew because I'd read it on chabad.com. Exile in the time of Sabbatai Zevi was a *spiritual mission* for those who lived in countries where they were being persecuted and oppressed. Because if you lived in persecution on the terrestrial plane, said Chabad, there was a *reason*. Your suffering was not in vain. You were here to look for and find holy sparks in darkness. Jews in exile, said chabad.com, had a *duty* to liberate holy sparks from evil.

I deduced that exile for Barbra – unwillingly taken from her home in Ethiopia and brought to a punishing, doglike Israel – experiencing *further* exile in our Rotary-fuelled Canadian basement – meant that she was here among us all to snuff out the evil.

I believed that she could liberate this Jew-boy from all fucked-up, racist things.

And I could help her, backwards, upside down: I could reverse the saviour fantasy.

§

I remember the first time I went to Joel's house, his Grade 10 sister was lying on the couch in a dark room with a wastebasket in front of her face.

'She has mono,' Joel said. 'From sucking face.'

Joel lived in one of the biggest houses in our neighbourhood. It was a fifteen-minute walk from school. He had a nanny because both of his parents worked full-time. Joel's nanny's name was Miriam and she was from Grenada. Miriam always called me 'sir' or 'young man' when me and Joel came in for lunch. Every single time, she made us Kraft Dinner. Joel ate his with ketchup. He didn't clean up his plate. I always brought mine to the sink and felt bad that Miriam was expected to clean.

'Joel,' Miriam always said. 'Look how this young man behaves.'

But I knew that I behaved poorly, too. I did not clean up every meal with my own mom.

Joel was the person who taught me the word *cunt*. He said it described a vagina succinctly.

'*Cunt* is succinct,' I parroted, not really knowing that word either but understanding instinctively. '*Cunt* is succinct. No ifs, ands, or buts.'

Joel started laughing. I laughed along. That day we rhymed *cunt* with *shunt*, *bunt*, and *runt*. The next day, I remember, I said *cunt* to Abigail. She was pretty young – me and Joel were in Grade 6 at the time and I don't even remember the context – but I know I didn't mean *cunt* as bad. *Cunt* was succinct! But Abigail instinctively felt like *cunt* was wrong. I guess we were both instinctive 'understanders.' Her face turned bright red at *cunt*. Then she shut her eyes and squeezed all the muscles in her body like she did sometimes at the table when she didn't want to eat.

'What's wrong with you, Abigail?' I remember I said. I watched my sister squeeze her face so hard until she seriously had to breathe.

Then, a few days later while we were in the car, Abigail said to my mother from the back seat: 'Mom, my cunt hurts.'

'What?' my mother exploded, all of a sudden speeding. I saw her neck skin go bright red, just like Abigail's had.

I knew that *cunt* to my mother meant something really bad.

'Your *vagina* hurts? You mean your *vulva*? Abigail, where did you *hear* that word?'

My mother was practically shrieking. She pulled us over abruptly. A car beeped behind us.

'It itches. Just a little,' Abigail said.

My mother spun around, purple-faced and still attached to her seat belt. Abigail stared at me.

Cunt was my shame. I couldn't look at my mother. 'I told her that. Sorry.'

'I don't want to *ever* hear you use that word. *Ever* again!'

My mother glared at me. She could not catch her breath. I said *sorry* again, in fact I said it a few more times and to Abigail, too, but my mother stayed mad at me for the whole day. I realized how brazen Joel was whenever he said the word *cunt*. Joel's father was a lawyer and his mother was a doctor who travelled to places like Johannesburg and Rio de Janeiro. I wanted to ask Joel why *cunt* was the worst word in the world for vagina.

'Miriam says it when she's on the phone, laughing. It's not *evil*,' Joel reported. '*Cunt. Scunt. Rashole.* All those words.'

When Miriam worked at Joel's house when we were in Grade 6, she always wore the same sack-shaped dress with pink roses. She wore yellow rubber gloves up to her elbows. In these gloves, I'd seen Miriam pinch Joel on his arm or his cheeks. It always seemed to me she meant, *I'm in charge of you.*

But after the lunch when I'd told Joel my *cunt* story and we were laughing, I saw Miriam pinch Joel *really* hard.

'I'm going to smack you so bad even your mother's not going to know how to fix it,' she said.

On our way back to school, Joel's cheek grew a welt that was purple and raised.

Joel said, 'She's not allowed to do that. I'm telling my dad.'

I felt weird, I felt guilty. I'd thought the word *cunt* was not evil. But I felt like Miriam now hated me, too.

§

It was the second week of August. Time was moving too fast. I kept texting her, *Come up. I'm awake. I'm awake!* I kept supplying her wine, leaving bottles on the bottom basement step. I kept trying to lure her back to me again. The night it worked, she was drunker than I'd ever seen her before.

'You know I'm the first Beta Israel refusenik,' she slurred. 'I told 'em to let me out of there.'

Beta Israel refusenik sounded heroic. I mean, I knew that the Israeli army was a really big deal.

Barbra plopped down on my bed. And all of a sudden, everything fell into place. *This* was the reason that her uncle said that she had one more chance. Barbra consciously objected and it was either prison or here.

'But how did you do it?' I asked breathlessly.

Barbra laughed. 'Bruh, I just told them what I really thought. I told 'em that I was a recipient of their fucking violent tactics. I told 'em I don't support bulldozing Arabs from their homes. They don't know what it's like to have no more home.'

I was holding my breath. I don't know what I was expecting. Jews knew what it was like to have no more home. My father had told me about the Kishinev pogrom, the original pogrom. Two of my grandparents' sisters died in the Holocaust.

'The Jews have *always* been under threat,' my father said. 'The Israeli army is our first, most successful self-defence.'

Purple-teethed and loose-legged, Barbra slid off my bed to the floor. Did she believe that the Jews had always been under threat?

'Put on your boots,' Barbra said. '*You* be my soldier.'

She was totally slurring. I was trying to make all the connections. The violent army, the first Beta Israel refusenik; demolitions and pogroms, Arabs and Sabbatians. My dad said, 'Moral army. The only democracy in the Middle East.'

'Come on, your army boots, bruh, right over there.'

I had Doc Martens under my bed. She wanted me to be the soldier, the soldier who took her from Ethiopia? Was this a part of her healing? Not being set out on the streets?

I felt sweat pouring out of my body from every tiny fucking follicle.

Barbra pulled off her T-shirt and rolled into the fetal position. 'Ask me where I'm from,' she said.

I put on my boots. It took time to lace them up.

'C'mon, put your boot on my back,' Barbra said.

I looked down at her half-naked shell shape, in those green satin shorts.

'Where's it? Wanna feel the boot!'

I put my boot in the middle of her polka-dot back.

'Ask me where I'm from,' Barbra said again.

I obeyed her directive. I stepped down a bit harder. Then I half-kicked and made her roll right onto her front. 'Where do you live, little girl?'

Barbra started laughing. She liked being booted. She liked *little girl*. She said, 'Tell me you're going to take me out of here.'

'Did you lose your mother, little girl?' I croaked.

Barbra rolled away from me. She rolled back to her belly, she rolled into my carpet. I put my boot back on her spine. I think she moaned. I had been thinking about her every single night since she'd appeared at our house with my father six weeks ago.

'I asked, did you lose your mother, little girl?'

Barbra writhed on the ground at the foot of my bed.

'If you lost your mother,' I went on, sticky-mouthed, 'you can just come home with me.'

My mother finally told us that she'd gotten a job – assistant professor of sociology at a college in Portland. She'd sat me and Abigail and Barbra all together at the kitchen table full of bagels and tuna fish salad and cheese. Abigail started crying right away that she wanted to go with my mother.

'I assume Dad knows this plan?' I asked. Oregon was over *five hours* by plane.

'Of course your father knows,' my mother snapped. She looked both sorry and like she felt sorry for me.

Barbra slid her chair over to Abigail's and put her arm around her. 'Ruth,' she said. 'Let's celebrate!'

The way Barbra said my mother's name, it sounded like *root*.

'You want a glass of wine? Okay, let's get a little wine.'

My mother stood up to distract herself. Barbra gave Abigail a napkin to wipe her nose. I felt both cold and excited. We would have this house nearly all to ourselves.

I pushed on Barbra's back with my boot to stop her writhing around. 'Why are you balled up, little girl? Don't be afraid. You can stretch out.'

'There is no such things as a moral army,' said my mother, 'even when they're saving Jews.'

'Be meaner,' Barbra echoed.

My hands formed into fists. My hands looked baby pink. 'Your mother said it was okay for you to come with me, little girl. Your father doesn't care. Your father is dead.'

I heard Barbra smothering her laughter in the carpet.

'You are a very pretty girl.' I was getting really angry. 'I'm going to take your picture, naked little girl, and show everyone.'

How could I be meaner? Her laughs sounded like crying. Abigail had stopped crying when my mother said that she could move to Portland, too. My mother had brought out a bottle of wine. Barbra and my mother laughed about tuna fish with wine. I bought these steel-toed Doc Martens at the army surplus store. *Root*. Barbra seemed way too happy for my mother.

'I'm lost. Take my picture. You can save me,' Barbra squeaked.

It occurred to me that she wasn't just going back to being the little girl orphan of Operation Solomon with the big bad soldier who carried her away. She was channelling Sarah, the Messiah's orphan-whore wife. Sabbatai Zevi was the first Jewish man in existence who decided that women should read the Torah and pray alongside the men. He said to the women: *I'll make you as happy as men.*

'I'm going to take you home, little girl, and keep you hidden in my burrow.'

'I dare you,' Barbra said as she arched her bum up to my boot. 'Take me.'

I smelled her wetness like moss in the room. My meanness got free. It unfurled at a quick pace. The soldier took her. He picked her little body up. She wanted more violence. Violence for an audience.

I crouched down, took a handful of her hair, and threaded it between my knuckles like I'd done the time before.

'No! That's not how you help me!' Barbra hissed.

She was in character. I abducted by force. I wanted to take her to the kitchen, fuck her smushed against the fridge. I wanted to hold her down in the family room, stomach to couch. Her basement, their bedroom: I wanted to desecrate this whole place. My mother didn't know how much Barbra drank wine without her. My mother wanted to just make things easy, it seemed. My father didn't know how much Barbra drank either. He had overdone Friday nights since she arrived. He did more prayers, we went through two glasses each. Barbra stored wine in the basement in brown paper bags. I counted. She must've had her own sources. Joel was a drug dealer. I did not procure two bottles a day.

I heard her stomach gurgling on my carpet. I released her hair for the second it took to slide my boot up to the ridge where her hairs met her neck. We were both sweating. My mother did not believe in air conditioning.

'Little girl, I have a lollipop in my car.'

Barbra couldn't move her head because of my boot. 'A lollipop?' she said.

'You should try to get up now,' I ordered.

But Barbara didn't try. She suddenly stopped writhing. She just lay there playing dead. I didn't know what had just happened. Was the lollipop wrong?

'Try to move,' I hissed. 'You have to try and fight.'

My mother had started packing up her stuff. Suitcases sat near our front door like roadblocks. Abigail had started throwing things away. She gave me one of her stuffies. 'I want you to remember me,' she said.

Barbra had suggested this scenario. *She* was the one who wanted it.

'Come on, I just want to give you a lollipop!' I hissed. I was starting to leave my character the soldier, looking down at Barbra's short shorts, the satin green crack of her ass. 'The lollipop is cherry. It's your favourite, little girl.'

My gut felt like a cave with gas roiling inside it. Barbara had a skin tag at the back of one ear. Abigail *had* to come back and visit me and Dad. She could keep her fucking stuffy. Paternal rights were the *law*.

'Little girl, answer me!'

But Barbra just lay there, dead in the ground. If she didn't start moving I'd end this game now. I unzipped my pants.

I repeated: 'Come lick the lollipop, Suicide Girl.'

I covered my dick in my shorts. My dick felt fucking huge. I wanted to tell her straight out: suck me. I was the abductor. Her saviour. I'd force her. I wanted her jaw dropped, tongue out, dragged into my bed.

'Come into my car, little girl. I'm going to take your picture.'

Men who took pictures of girls were so fucking creepy.

Pictures in their bathing suits, pictures in their satin short shorts. I wanted her to get off the floor. I wanted to force her to suck me. I felt evil. Immoral. I saw her eyelids twitch.

'Come *on*. Fuck. Get up. Are you going to come to my car?'

She was a lump on my floor. I nudged her head with my boot.

'Answer me!'

'I'm not lost anymore,' Barbra finally said. 'I'm not a little girl anymore.'

Barbra rolled onto her back. She lay there looking up at me.

All of a sudden I felt prickling wet shame. I was like Joel. My mother was leaving my father. My sister was leaving our childhood home. All those Jews left their homes, homes bull-dozed by the army, believing that exile finally was through.

'I'm sorry,' I whispered.

'You don't have to be.'

Both her eyes were electric. I still felt so bad. I knew if she stayed there like that, I'd cum in her face. That was upside down. Fuck. I wanted to stop. God, I did not want to cum in her face. Unless she wanted me to cum in her face.

'Jew-boy, just keep going, okay?'

My veins felt like a blood web all over my face. Spiders dripped from their sacs, all their thin newborn legs. God, I felt like the creepiest of creepy abductors. I had to hold my cock down.

'I've never had an orgasm, little girl.'

Still covering my cock, I unzipped and let my jeans down halfway.

'Yeah, that's good.' Barbra smiled.

'I never ever ejaculated, I'm sorry,' I croaked.

'Yeah, yeah, just keep going like that.'

Barbra had thick black gunk weight on her eyelashes. She got up to her elbows. She twitched.

'I want you to cum so hard you don't know what hit you,' Barbra said.

I had a boot on either side of her waist. I was the soldier. The soldier who had taken her from home. Barbra dropped her head backwards. Nipples vibrating, headless. I stared at her not-oblong tits.

'You're going to make me cum…' I said.

Barbra cackled and lifted her head back up. I did not recognize my voice. The game began again.

'Suck me, little girl,' I said weakly. 'Or I'm not taking you home.'

Barbra licked her bird's speckled teeth.

'Suck my cock *now* or I won't take you home.'

'What makes you think that I want to go home?'

Her cheeks were flushed, her eyes like two oysters. Tongue gloss, all this strange mush sheen. I wanted to turn her to mush everywhere. I did not want her to ever go home again.

'Suck it,' I said.

I dropped my underwear down. Took my hand off myself. Bobbing and stuck, red-dicked in front of her crossed eyes.

'Fuck you, Jew-boy.'

My gut lurched. I made her. Don't call me Jew-boy. I forced her mush mouth to my dick head. She cackled again. I crouched down toward her tits. This was a fight. I put one sweaty hand on the back of her head. All her hairs twisted around my two thumbs. I felt angry. I thought of domestic abuse. Then I slid deeper in, pushed myself hard at her lips. She pretended to gag but she opened for me. She was *laughing* at me. Her oyster eyes roamed. Did she read that whole book?

She opened her jaw. Felt like roots in her mouth, felt like fern tongues and shoots. My legs were on fire, she sucked it, my whole body taut.

'Little girl, little girl, I'm going to cum … '

My whole body pumped like an overworked heart. But then, rapidly, somehow, she ejected my cock. I looked down at her lips, the gushes of spit. My cock was slick, yellowish, wrinkled near the head. I wanted her back but she slithered away.

Barbra, I'm sorry, I wanted to say.

'Take me home,' Barbra murmured, back on her belly. 'I wanna go home. Nothing is good here. I wanna go home.'

I heard myself make this one awful noise. I did not ever want to be a soldier in my life. Abductors are people who've found their worst side.

'Did you hear me, bruh? I said, *take me home*.'

I squatted low and hovered an inch off her back. Like some kind of he-man, I jerked myself off. Bird's-eye view. *Where* was home? This felt like the beginning all over again. My asshole confusion. She drank way too much.

'Can I cum, Barbra? Please?'

My thighs were on fire. Just me and her in this home. I used my free hand to pinch the side of her tit. She lifted up from that side so I could get my whole hand on it. She was superhuman. She read more than me. Her nipple burned through my palm. My hard cock touched the back of her ass. I needed both hands.

'Barbra. *Bar-ba-ra*.' I heard myself saying her name.

She had ruptured my force field for seven weeks.

'Cum,' she hissed. '*Cum*.'

I jerked over her back. I spit from above. I was still the abductor. I took her right to the plane. *Bar-ba-ra. Bar-bruh*.

She was not kicked out of the army, that's what my father believed.

My mother said, 'Everyone has to respect what she needs.'

But I knew the truth of her story. She was righteous. She'd been punished. *This* was her healing. I was doing what she wanted. I wanted her to suck me all over again. One more day. Every night. Barbra mumbled in Hebrew. I covered her ear with my palm and stared down at her ass. It rippled like a lizard in her short shorts, cleaving me.

'You are in love with me, Jew-boy,' Barbra said.

Yeah, was *this* was what love felt like? The urge to puncture and bury? Lines of blood boiling inside your brain?

My knees pinned her sides. I lodged there, that tight spot, her ass ridge, and I pumped. I dug my knees into the carpet. Barbra started shaking, popping her back. Yeah, I was in love. I pinched her tit, both her tits, my white cock stuck between her satin green crack. I muffled out *love*. She fucked the ground moaning. She kept my cock stuck in the ridge of her, shaking and bulging. I shot like a squid on her slippery back.

Cum does not dissolve in the valley. It sits and it sticks. It assimilates.

§

Barbra wrote all over that thousand-page book, smearing her chicken-scratch Hebrew in the margins. She left it on her pillow in the basement like a parting shot.

§

I was the one in the end who had to tell Abigail the truth. She thought my mother's job in Portland meant that our parents were going to live apart but stay married. Abigail was immature for someone almost twelve years old. That was my sole diagnosis for my sister. My mother had had Abigail labelled with sensory processing disorder. My father had always said that she would just grow out of things. Sometimes I felt like there was a whole other family in my house – a silent shadow family that existed, that took the place of my mom and my dad, Abigail and me. I wasn't sure, when I was younger, if that was real or a dream.

'Mom and Dad will be better apart,' I told Abigail. 'No more stupid, endless fights.'

'So, is Barbra gonna stay?' My sister was looking at me funny.

'I don't know. How should I know? Why do you like her so much?'

'You mean, why do *you*?'

Abigail reminded me of the Mad Hatter, with her front two buck teeth and oblong-shaped head.

'I know why *I* like her,' Abigail said.

'Yeah? Go ahead. Tell me.'

'Because Barbra doesn't know anything about me or my problems and she still likes me anyway.'

Sometimes Abigail and Barbra went to the park together after dinner. Barbra pushed Abigail, too big for the swing, trying to launch her, I thought, round the whole rusted structure.

'I don't get why you act like such a douche around her,' my sister said. 'Why don't you just act like yourself? I like Barbra because she makes me more *me*.'

It took me a second to understand what my sister was saying. Like, it took me a second to grasp in totality this concept she expressed. Because something exactly like that had occurred to me too – I mean, in what Abigail said first, not me being a douche. My sister reported that Barbra liked her *without* the knowledge of her problems. Bull's-eye. This was my problem, too. Barbra thought I was a completely blank slate. My mother said there was no such thing as a blank slate. Barbra had entered our house at the beginning of the summer when she knew absolutely *nothing* about me, nothing, in fact, about any of us. And we didn't know her either – how she felt, who she was, what in the world she was actually thinking. And so some kind of lopsided, criss-crossed *merger* had taken place. For Abigail, this was growth. But for me, it was – I don't know – *violation*. Or maybe this was just the fucking human condition. Maybe it was also an unfolding emotional crime. She named me Jew-boy. She told me to hurt her. Barbra drank up all our wine. Barbra thought that my family's preconceived notions – our natures/our nurtures – could just be burned to the ground.

For *her*? Who was she? The fucking Messiah?

She was a Jew! We were Jews, too.

And while my sister experienced Barbra's presence as benevolence, what I got by the end was dissolution.

Present

She came back for me the first Monday in March, the day that I quit school for good. The family room was my study now, coffee table stacked with books. Candles in all her old wine bottles lined the two window ledges, marked with wart lines of red and black wax. Our L-shaped leather couch doubled most nights as my bed. Ash spotted the bricks of our fireplace.

My mother still blamed my father for Barbra. She said the real crime was when *the helpers don't help*. My father did not defend himself anymore. 'We made a mistake,' he said to me, standing in my bedroom doorway, soon after Barbra left. 'All of us, everyone, we all made mistakes.' But apportioning blame to 'everyone' – who? Bob Cunningham, the soldier, my mother, her wine? – was a strange way, I thought, of understanding what had happened. I knew, in his gut, that my father blamed me.

In and out of therapy, I'd named Barbra my molester. *Molester* trumped *bitch*. *Molester*, I thought, was more cognizant of both her power and my eventual retreat. *Molester* soothed me nightly, too, throughout this motherless, father-driven, seven-year cycle of blame.

§

The shyster squatted in front of my books. His blousy beige shirt opened one button too low. He had a leathery breastbone, cattle ribs. I could not believe she actually liked this type of thing. Eventually, he picked out *My People Shall Live* from my

Palestine stack. The shyster liked hot young Leila Khaled with her gun. I seriously could not believe that this guy was her *boyfriend*. His greasy salt-and-pepper braid hung between his shoulder blades. He looked like he would have faded tattoos, some secret green-bleeding feather, limp on his breast.

I paced behind the coffee table as the shyster used *My People Shall Live* to pulverize some kind of herb and fill a little carved, clay South American pipe.

'You know, she likes a little hash to relax.'

God, I hated his lisping and slithery French accent. It was all coming back in this dizzying gust: Barbra's need for me to be sucked into her shit. She was upstairs in our house in the shower alone. Still a drug fiend, a wine head, a sexual freak. God, was she back here for a renewed bout of hallucinogenic sex torture? Faux-masochistic, violent bitch! Look, I know it wasn't good for me to curse her in my head. I'd thrown *bitch* out five years ago. Dr. Bornstein said that it wasn't good for my healing to fixate on bad thinking, i.e., to call someone who hurt me misogynist names. Bornstein tended to agree with my father that I tended to inner-exaggerate.

But I did *not* want her back here. Bitch, for seven years I'd been *fine*.

I'd burned her fucking messianic book alongside my family's whole Israel Operation Saviour Fantasy thread.

My girlfriend for the past two years had worked really hard with me to exorcise Barbra's elemental presence from my thinking. I knew that *elemental* was a way better concept than *bitch*. *Elemental* trumped *molester*. *Elemental* was *it*. Ariane said that I had a lot of anger during sex. She said she thought I pounded to get at what I thought I'd been denied. In truth, Ariane only knew about a third of the story of me and Barbra, but she insisted that I had to get rid of this feeling that I wanted to subdue or somehow overpower a woman.

Ariane said: *There is nothing inside a woman that is denying you something.*

Ariane said: *I'm not a trap door. I'm* meeting *you.*

Ariane worked with me during sex to change my 'bad thinking.' She actually called it 'traumatized thinking' – a need to smother all my bad thoughts with sex. Ariane said I had textbook sex addiction, that my shame from Barbra and the failed way it ended meant, in fact, that I hated myself.

For two years, okay, this is what me and Ariane talked about. I mean, this is what we worked on during sex. I didn't tell Ariane that it was not always therapeutic. In fact, sometimes it even made me feel worse. Like, Ariane would tell me in sex to go slower and why, and then harder and why, how to lick her, how to suck her and why and why. I secretly did not always subscribe to her method, even though I did like that we had a lot of sex.

What Ariane fixated mostly on about my relationship with Barbra was that she thought that I thought that Barbra *wanted* to be submissive because Barbra explicitly told me to hurt her.

'I was mistaken about that,' Ariane deduced. 'Barbra was obviously *not* a submissive.' Ariane said that what we did was s/m 101. She said what Barbra did is called 'topping from the bottom.'

Uh, does 'topping from the bottom' mean you make up all the rules? I wanted to ask her. Does 'topping from the bottom' mean that the knife is always truly yours?

I did not tell Ariane about our specific scripts. I did not tell Ariane about what truly happened at the ending. I told her my scar was from surgery when I was fourteen after I broke my collarbone. I told her, in general, that Barbra asked me to do something and I did it. I told her that we didn't really have to say *yes* or *no*. It was a system, I explained, of complicit synchronicity.

Ariane scoffed. She continually tried to school me. In sex, she said, the woman must lead.

'This is ancient knowledge. Stuff the Tantrics believed.'

Did the Tantrics believe that a turned-on and traumatized woman could be *actually* violent? Tantric is outdated, I thought. What did they know about consent?

Ariane assured me that my true self was not chauvinistic. She said that all real men worshipped cunt.

Ariane said, 'If you love cunt, you actually have to know how to treat it. If you love cunt, you have to know your way around its complex abyss.'

Sometimes I thought Ariane only liked me because I made her feel worshipped. I loved Ariane's body. She was long-armed, big-nippled, bluish-skinned. When we had sex, I usually licked her pussy for an hour. Between Barbra and Ariane, I'd *practised* cunt-licking. Girls always said that they loved my way of licking. I always signed my name on their thighs. I licked them and tricked them, massaged them and slapped them. Pussy foam, pussy oil. I liked period pains. I got off being smothered. I liked to see girls get really wild. Licked-open cunts liked to get really wild.

I told the cunt to sit on my face.

I said to the cunt, *please hump my whole head.*

I loved cunts lodged with matter. I loved a maw full of cunt on my pillowcase.

Ariane said she thought that I needed female *camaraderie.*

She said she thought that I still needed to work on seeing girls as truly *equals*. She said it was good that I ended my friendship with Joel during high school. She said that Joel was an entitled little prick. Ariane said that chauvinists needed to affirm themselves in groups. She said, that's the meaning of *brotherhood*.

Barbra called me *bruh*. She anointed me *Jew-boy* and *bruh*.

The shyster offered me a drag of his South American pipe. It had a carved face on the bowl of a squat man wearing a hat. The pipe tasted like it had been soaked in cologne.

I tried to smoke and to focus on the situation at hand. I tried to focus on the fact that my elemental molester was back, that she brought this treacherous Frenchman with her. I could not focus. Ariane was going to be here soon. God, Ariane and Barbra were going to meet. I smoked and I hedged. I smoked and I hedged. I imagined her slithering upstairs in our fungal-scum bathtub. Why'd she ignore me for seven fucking years?

'Did you know that Leila Khaled hijacked those planes because she needed her father's attention?'

I was speaking too quickly.

The shyster laughed. 'She told me you often got angry like this.'

'And did you know that Leila Khaled had plastic surgery before her second hijacking *without an anaesthetic*,' I went on, 'because she said she could subordinate her personal pain in service of the liberation of her people?'

The shyster smirked. 'So what does that have to do with *Papa*?'

I passed back his pipe. I wanted to pitch it. 'Leila said, and I quote, "I've always wanted to know people who love others more than themselves."'

The shyster made an *ah* sound that reminded me of my mom.

'Tell me, what doctor, in his right mind, would do a nose job without anaesthetic? What kind of a father would actually *do* that surgery?'

The shyster looked amused. 'So you doubt the truth?'

'Yeah, man! That's what I do.'

I was pacing back and forth, stiff-kneed. The world disappointed Leila Khaled. God, I wanted to bust this guy's paternal amusement. Had Barbra told him that I was some naive little Jew-boy whose house they could ransack, whose dad they could blackmail, whose shit they could five-finger scrape from the pipes?

The shyster looked through another one of my stacks. My Palestine stack was in the middle of my Holocaust stacks. All my Holocaust books had been beaten up and defaced.

I did not know about Leila and the *Nakba* until I was twenty years old.

I'd been accepted late to York for a double major in English Lit and Jewish Studies and I'd just kept going, from undergrad to grad. My mother had encouraged me from her post across the country. She'd probably told the dean that I'd written my high school exams in and out of hospital beds. My mother always said that I was a very sensitive reader. She said that that would be a shame to waste.

At York, though, at first, I felt *desensitized*. Maybe from all the head drugs that my father made sure I was taking every morning. But I am not lying or hedging when I say that my desensitization was totally through after I encountered the York University Arab Students Association. In the rotunda, you could stand there for an hour in front of their video screens. You could stand there and watch the crowds of young men and boys throwing rocks at IDF tanks. Faces prematurely aged, faces contorted. Jaws detached for screaming. The First Intifada, the Second, and maybe the Third. Kids my age bleeding from holes in their lips, cracks in their foreheads. I saw rubber bullets, clouds of tear gas, bodies smouldering and falling through warped Stars of David. I took all the ASA pamphlets. I went to their websites. I read about Fatah, Hamas, the Liberation of Palestine. And I swear, I felt this fucking caesura – something so huge was missing in me. I saw how the Jewish Students Association in the rotunda booked counter-tables, played TV screens with their own grim displays: spray-painted swastikas in Europe's last Jewish graveyards, a *get out kikes* screed mailed to a Jewish school in Montreal. The JSA even published ads in the student newspaper calling the ASA Holocaust deniers. I was privy to this stuff in the Jewish Studies lounge – kids saying they were just opposed to material that they said 'glorified Hamas.' It is against the charter to preach violence against Jews at the university, they said. What I didn't understand was this so-called, assumed primal animosity between Arabs and Jews in and out of the rotunda, even though, yes, I understood that war between them was ongoing…

But, like, why as a Jew are you opposed to someone just because that someone opposes you?

Tell me what exactly it is, I posted in some JSA chat room, *that you Jew-boys are so threatened by? Arabs are not the ones knocking your ancestors' stones down! Are you threatened by the Palestinian Right of Return? Or is it too painful to admit that the Israeli army murdered four Arab children playing on a beach?*

I did not believe that my Jewish Studies comrades cared about those kids. I did not believe my father cared either. I wanted to talk to the ASA about this. What was missing when we were not mourning dead kids? I got JSA hate mail sent to my York U account. I was told that Hamas wanted to drive Jews into the sea, and if I didn't believe that, I should go live with ISIS. When I asked the ASA about ISIS, they told me I should probably stop visiting them. Then, because rejection often happens in succession, Professor Sugarman kicked me out of her Interwar Jewish Lit because I questioned if the way she was talking about Bruno Schulz's masochism was legit.

Later, I consulted Jim, and Jim reiterated, 'Yes, Schulz was a textbook masochist.'

Look, I *knew* that my anger was all over the place. Sometimes I thought we should just all return to the fucking ice age.

Jim helped me out when I was rejected like this. I spent a lot of time at the store. Jim advocated sharing knowledge to combat all things. He prescribed me a general Arab literature primer. I read novels by Mahfouz, Yasmina Khadra, Nawaal El-Sadaawi. Then Jim ordered me a collection of Ghassan Kanafani as I read *My People Shall Live* and *Orientalism*. And yes, I *knew* that Leila Khaled was a problematic hero – that hijacking two planes was a sure way of losing international support for your cause. But nose job or not, I got the raw injustice. Leila and her family were expelled from Haifa by force in 1948. Their land was not for sale nor purchased. This was violent expulsion, a.k.a. ethnic cleansing. Entire Arab towns and Arab neighbourhoods: gone. I was taught that 1948 was a war of independence.

Jim recommended books by Israeli historians. I learned that the founder of Zionism was a charismatic wife-beater. I learned that he proposed a homeland for the Jews in *Uganda*. I learned that Zionism began as literal science fiction. I learned that in pre-war Europe, the Zionists and Socialists were *opposed*. In interwar Europe, Zionism was seen by most Jews as *fringe*.

Jim was the one during the first year of my master's who pointed me toward the work of Ka-Tzetnik 135633. This was after I told him how Sugarman was making us write about *The Painted Bird* in tandem with *Night*.

'Maybe you'll find this fellow an antidote,' Jim said as he handed me a plastic-wrapped pulp paperback called *House of Dolls*. On the cover was a faceless, breasty woman in a ripped-open prison gown.

'An antidote to *what*?' I asked.

Jim smiled too easily. 'Don't quote me,' he said, 'but an antidote to the way the Holocaust is taught to you young Jews.'

Above the woman's cleavage, there was tattooed: *Feld-Hure 135633*.

I'd learned about the Holocaust in Hebrew school. I'd learned that Jewish people all over Europe were targeted, shipped, enslaved, and gassed to death. I'd learned the number six million. Jews were nearly *annihilated*. I'd learned in Hebrew school, too, about the ragged survivors. I'd learned that after the war, they needed a land to belong. I was taught that Israel was their empty Nirvana.

Jim said, 'We have to examine the validity of the gas chambers.'

'The *validity*?'

'*You* tell *me*. Who counted the bodies? The British? The Americans? I don't believe the Americans. We have to draw our own conclusions, us thinking men.'

'Uh…'

'*House of Dolls*,' Jim continued, 'is a *very* unique book. An example of the first wave of these pseudo-truths peddled, which has become an industry, as you know.'

Wait. My friend Jim was a Holocaust denier?

Jim winked at me. 'I'll give you a little Faurisson next.'

For the first time since I'd known him, Jim made me feel really weird. But I bought *House of Dolls* and I read it three times in a row. I read about Daniela, Ka-Tzetnik's sister, forced into prostitution in Auschwitz.

Daniela was treated like a dog.

Ka-Tzetnik survived Auschwitz and wrote *House of Dolls* soon after he arrived in Israel. I learned that there was this detention centre near Haifa after World War II where new refugees like Ka-Tzetnik were processed and held. I read that people were sprayed in that centre with DDT.

I thought about Barbra's head measured and taped.

I never went back to Jim's bookstore again.

'Would you like some?' The shyster offered me his fresh pipe, outstretched.

I shook my head no. I'd already had too much. Toxic smoke singed my throat hairs. My throat felt like rope fray. God, this was a relapse. Was this a relapse and I could not admit it? It felt just like the first time all over again.

I heard her barefoot galloping downstairs. Shit churned in my gut. My tongue trapped in a trench.

And she stood there, six feet of her, back in the doorway. Short hair slicked, no bra, in my T-shirt. A ratty yellow towel knotted round her like a skirt.

'I wanted to see the old room,' Barbra announced.

Water drops slid down the side of her face.

'Very good, very good,' the shyster said.

Barbra trotted down the three steps to the family room.

Her tits bounced. Her knees cracked. She sat right on his lap. I felt sick, I felt triggered by her back here again. The shyster's hand clamped on her thigh. Ariane called that part the flank. Moon-shaped wet spots spread out from her pits. That was *my* shirt. Pellets of snow hit the screen doors.

'When is he going to forgive me?' Barbra whispered.

The shyster's claw travelled under her towel. I was having a relapse. She put her mouth near his collar. She started licking his neck. Loose white hairs electrified round his forehead.

'Stop it,' I croaked.

It was happening again. Her tongue was out, she was licking for salt. The shyster slowly nudged up her towel. I remembered the feel of her burning goose flesh. My neck tightened in pain. Her licks turned robotic.

'Stop,' I repeated.

God, I loved her hot fat. She'd lost too much weight. I wanted to hear all about the last seven years. Her tongue's doggy licking, my cock got so hard. My father said I would forget about her one day. Bornstein said I had to forgive her one day. But the goddess who had indoctrinated me was now moaning in our family room on top of a geezer and I still felt the need to fucking fuck her. Or love her.

God, I hated the endless loop of this thing.

§

Ariane lunged at me at the front door. Her icy nose hit my cheek.

'My brakes froze. I need a hot drink,' she said.

Snow melted on her coat and all-weather bike pants. Did she notice their duffle bag slumped on the floor? Did she notice the haze that had slipped over my head? We walked to the kitchen, cold hand stuck in hand.

'So, what happened with Sugarman today?'

I still hadn't looked Ariane in the eyes. We'd talked about that a few weeks ago – how she didn't like it when I didn't look her in the eyes when we first saw each other.

'I quit and she quit,' I reported, robotic.

'*Fuck*. That absolutely sucks.'

I knew she'd imagined us in the States together next year, both of us doing our PhDs. Ariane was the one who'd encouraged me to focus solely on the life and work of Ka-Tzetnik 135633 even as Sugarman said that I had to be careful not to smear Holocaust fiction a priori by ignoring survivors' textual multiplicities.

At first, I'd wanted to call my thesis *The Hoax of Early Holocaust Literature*, and Sugarman, my advisor, had refused it.

'The word *hoax* is a trigger. You know that,' Sugarman said.

'But I'm appropriating *hoax*,' I said. 'Like the so-called ASA Holocaust deniers.'

'Come *on*, we've been through all this, like, a million times,' Sugarman said.

I didn't tell Ariane this part, that Sugarman months ago had started flagging me to campus security.

'Barbra's back,' I said quickly instead.

Ariane stared at me. I turned away.

'I don't know why she's here. With some guy. I don't totally believe it myself.'

'Look at me,' Ariane ordered.

I couldn't control the muscles in my jaw.

'Are you okay, or no?'

'You mean with her back here?'

'No. I mean with *everything*.'

The hanging light in our kitchen heat-flooded my face.

'You look like you're happy she's here, if we're being honest.'

My smile was morbid anxiety.

'You can fuck anyone you want, you know that, right?'

'Ariane,' I hissed. 'This is *not* about *that*.'

Ariane was the one who said we were polyamorous. She thought that her being so-called supportive of whatever I had to 'explore' solved every other problem between us. But I hated these terms: *supportive, explore*. I hated fucking polyamory, too. I preferred lying. Lying was better. It was closer to the truth.

'Hey, look at me, *babe*. We've talked about you fucking other girls.'

God, I hated it when Ariane called me *babe*. I hated it when she made a big deal about my sex drive. I didn't want other girls when I was with Ariane. Fuck. I *really* wished she hadn't come over tonight. Ariane always wanted to talk about why I'd never dated white girls, why I only liked women of colour. She liked listing my roster between Barbra and her: Erica, Ellery, Kawai, and Lisette. Ariane said that she thought that I thought women of colour were more oppressed or some-thing, and that that meant I thought I had more power over them. She said that this process operated *consciously* in me. She said I had seriously unchecked white privilege.

'White privilege is not invisible,' Ariane said.

'I know that, I get that,' I agreed explicitly.

I told Ariane that I knew white men needed to step back-wards, acknowledge their privilege, and practise listening in their own lane. I told Ariane that my relationship with Barbra had politicized me.

'Explain to me why you've desired women of colour, espe-cially Black women,' Ariane said, 'as a kind of exploitation.'

I rolled my eyes. We could never get further than this. S/M 101 was not exploitation. I could not do Ariane's math to completion in my head. I mean, I knew that something she said about me was true. And I knew that it involved US history or something – like when I read about white slave masters absolving their guilt for raping their black female slaves because they said they *tempted* them. I knew about the stereo-type of the black Jezebel. It was *totally* fucked. White men were 100 percent guilty of shooting trauma into Black women. But I seriously did not know how to fit myself into all this. Like, wasn't my relationship with Barbra different than a white slave master raping? Was or was not our system of instinctive complicity consent?

Ariane always had to make me feel my so-called negative status as a white man – which she said trumped my Jewishness – even though I know she loved how I made her feel: how much I was in touch with my feelings, how much I was in touch with hers. I was the first guy to ever make her come multiple-y.

'I'm not fucking anyone except *you*, Ariane.'

'Bullshit,' Ariane said, and walked away from me.

God, I felt guilty. Was I actually guilty? Why was I feeling white-man guilty right now? All three of them were down there in the family room. I plugged my ears so that I would not hear them. Barbra came back and Ariane *just walked in*. Ariane did not understand what this was doing to me! Fuck. This person who'd fucked up my life had just flat-out returned. I scratched my arms. *Molester.* My throat felt weird. *Molester. Molester* trumped *Jezebel.* I wished Ariane would stop playing these mind games with me.

'Why do you think that Barbra is the molester,' Bornstein had repeatedly asked me, 'if you call yourself the abuser?'

I did not have a fucking pat answer for *why*. The doctor was the one who was supposed to help me with that. I showed up every week for years and I did not feel any different. Now, seven years ended. Fuck, seven years: gone.

Bornstein, our sex games fed my sex addiction.

Instinctive, collective. No *yes* and no *no*.

I found myself bracing the door to the family room, arms out like twigs. Like Jesus, a failure.

Bornstein, *I* was the abuser because *I* was the one who acted out. The molester, right there, she only initiated me.

'That is *not* the definition of molester,' Bornstein coolly informed me. 'Molestation is *unwanted*. It's a priori wrong. Initiation is *not* what it means.'

Barbra sat crossed-legged and happy in the L-joint of the couch, somehow using the towel to cover her crotch. Ariane sat to her left, farthest from the peasant-bloused shyster.

'This is my girlfriend, Ariane Chan,' I announced from the top of the family room stairs.

'I told them my name,' snapped Ariane.

The shyster passed Barbra a freshly lit pipe. I watched Barbra wiggle with it over to Ariane.

'You don't look Jewish at all,' Barbra said.

Ariane laughed. I thought, defaulting to coy. Barbra kept moving closer to my girlfriend, sidling right up beside her, smoke leaking out of her lips. I felt dizzy, revolted. It all seemed in slo-mo. The leaked smoke made a helix. Ariane opened her mouth. Barbra fed her the pipe. My throat shrank to the size of a tube.

I thought, abusers and molesters are supposed to be together.

Jezebel and Jew-boy ripping the system.

I remembered when Barbra said to me: I am ruining other girls for you for life.

Bornstein, this is the definition of molester: slick ruination raining all over me.

§

At our last Friday-night dinner before my mother left, Barbra looked strange. She wore a ruffled, white-stitched, kind of Victorian dress.

'Looks great on you,' said my mother, filling our goblets with wine.

Barbra screwed her hands together and stared at her plate.

'We're sending you two off in style,' my father boomed. 'Chicken from Dominion, just like my mother's. I like a little *schmaltz*, me and Abbi like a little *schmaltz*. The kid's gonna miss me. She likes the way I dress it up with *schmaltz*.'

God, I wished he would shut up. Even Abigail grimaced.

'Well, kids, what do you say?'

My father handed Abigail the knife for the challah. My mother unpacked the side dishes of beets and potatoes. Barbra's fingers interlaced like she was crushing something.

'I will light the candles tonight,' Barbra said, standing up. 'For Ruth.'

'Good, good. For Ruth? Fine. She needs matches.'

My father twisted around and reached into the drawer of the hutch. Barbra had told me that there was no such thing as racism in Ethiopia. Ethiopia, she said, had had no problem with Jews. My father pitched a pack of matches at Barbra. This was my mother's and Abigail's last night at home so we were eating in the dining room.

'I'm not cooking, I'm not lifting a finger,' my mom had said.

'It was only in Israel,' Barbra had told me, 'where people were first ever racist to us. They called us names. They called me *kushi*. Israel was a disappointment,' she'd said.

I smelled Barbra's sweat under her Victorian sleeves. The chicken stunk. My mother looked sad.

'She know the words? You need help? Abbi, help Barbra.'

'*Daddy*, no,' Abigail whined.

'*Regga*,' Barbra mumbled. She closed her eyes. She seemed sluggish. I knew she'd been drinking all day again.

'Come on, *Baruch atah Adonai…*'

'Stop!' my mother said to my father. 'Stop speaking.'

Stop drinking.

My father was compulsive. He had to cough to shut himself up. Barbra towered in silence above all of us. I looked at my sister. She looked like she was going to cry. I could hear mites in the air. I could hear the air beat. Then Barbra cupped both her hands over her eyes. The knuckles pointed out. It was as if her body shifted left. Our five-pointed chandelier hung like a crown over her head.

'I want to thank God.' Barbra started speaking so slowly. 'I thank the mother in the house, the mother who takes care of her children more than herself.'

Barbra paused. The light hit her knuckles, illuminated her hairs. 'The mother who now also takes care of herself.'

My father coughed again loudly. 'What kind of a *brucha* is this?'

Barbra let her hands drop. But her eyes were still closed. Her eyelids were vibrating. My father could not be silent for this.

'She's got the matches right in front of her. What's she *doing*?' my father hissed.

I wanted to die. It occurred to me that what we'd done in my room was *dehumanizing*.

Abbi closed her eyes just like Barbra. She fluttered her eyelids. My mother inched her chair closer. Female silence wove a strange fuzz. I felt a ball in my throat made of porcelain.

'Come on, Ruth, this shouldn't take so long.'

'Daddy, be *quiet*,' Abigail said.

I swallowed. It was difficult. In silence, she swayed. My throat started to hurt. It was sweltering.

'Barbra,' my mother said softly, 'is everything okay?'

Abruptly, Barbra opened her eyes. She broke off a match from the package and swiped it too hard. The flame of it flared up triple-size.

'Easy now,' my father laughed. 'Don't burn the place down.'

We all stared at the flame. Barbra stared inward. With one lit-up and sinuous hand over the other, Barbra pitched toward the candles and started to chant.

'*Abeytu Anteh Baruk Neh, Amlakachin yezemenat Nigus …* '

I breathed in and out. My skin prickled. All her gruffness was gone.

'*Yemedanin Menged Yemeese Tilin …* '

Barbra lit both of the candles, eyes glossy. Heart blood pumped inside my eardrums.

'*Be-meseeh Eyesus, i'su Buruk New, Ameyn.*'

Then Barbra blew out the match. My father was finally silent. A stream of smoke rose to our dining room ceiling. Abigail mouth-breathed. Barbra covered both eyes again.

'Aren't we going to say the Hebrew prayer, too?'

My mother glared at my father. She had left him com - pletely. I tried to swallow the little white ball in my throat again and again.

'Barbra, thank you. That was so beautiful. I'm so sorry about the interruptions,' my mother said.

My mother gave a little pull on Barbra's white dress. Barbra's arms fell limp and then she sat down beside me. Her eyes were now soap-bubble glossy as she nodded at each one of us in succession. First my mother, then Abigail, then my father, then me.

'What was *that?*' my father said.

'Fuck, *Dad*, don't you know when you've been *blessed?*' I found my real voice. It felt like a fountain.

My father grunted. We sat in this stultifying silence.

No one can lead anyone out of oppression.

'My parents taught me,' Barbra said quietly, 'to chant in Ge'ez.'

'Will you teach it to me?' Abigail asked.

Barbra shyly smiled and nodded. My mother exaggeratedly blew air out of her mouth to relax. She made a quick prayer over the wine. She told Abigail to cut up the challah. My father picked up chicken with his hands. I realized that Barbra had covered her eyes again.

I felt her hunched over in my peripheral vision. I stared at my plate. I knew that this was not still a part of her Shabbos. I got this hollow, cold feeling. She missed her real parents. Her real country. Barbra missed real *Judaism.*

It was as if she'd been forced into exile by lies.

'I had a good time here, Ruth, thank you,' Barbra whispered, face hidden, to the tablecloth.

My mother made a guttural sound. She slung her arm tightly around Barbra's shoulder.

I wanted to help Barbra, too, but I felt like I had to cry.

'It was the Rotary's idea for you to even be here,' my mother said quickly, her voice strangled. 'I'm so, so sorry I have to leave…'

'Ruth,' my dad choked.

'Thank you, Dr. Cohn,' Barbra got out, head bowed.

'Okay, that's fine, you can eat now,' my dad said, his voice also strained.

Abigail instinctively got up from the table to pee.

'We were not poor in Ethiopia,' I heard Barbra whisper to my mother, her head tucked in like a swan's.

My thigh twitched. I felt bad. This felt paralyzing.

She went on, 'We had meals like this.'

My mother stroked Barbra arms. The candles melted onto Bubie Marsha's gold candlesticks.

'It's okay,' my mother whispered, 'if you're not okay with all this.'

Barbra nodded and took a deep, sharp inhale. She finally took her hands off her face. Her eyes were backlit. Our family was hewed right in half. Wax balls disfigured the candles like pimples. My father resumed with his chicken. My mother poured us more wine.

I reached for Barbra's hand under the table. She let me have it. I pulsed on repeat. Motherless. Fearless. *Buruk New, Ameyn.*

§

The scalp-tattooed woman behind the counter asked if we were legal. Barbra handed the woman her crinkled Israeli ID. I flipped through the binder of half-naked hula-hoop girls.

'I'm here to get pierced,' Barbra said.

The woman put a clipboard in front of us on the counter.

She had foamy green eyeliner under her eyes and a skull on her skull, dotted with follicles.

'Where, hon?' she asked.

'Clitoris,' Barbra said.

I coughed. I kept coughing until I could not breathe.

'You probably should ask your boyfriend to leave.'

'I will.' Barbra smiled. 'But first he's paying for it.'

The woman gave Barbra a sheet of paper and pointed at a laminated contract page. 'Clit's right here,' she said.

I stuffed my cold hand in my pocket for my father's credit card.

Barbra stared at a smudged black line drawing of a vagina. She traced her finger around the vulva, in and out between the lips.

The woman handed Barbra back her ID. 'You gotta check all the boxes and sign for consent.'

Barbra pointed at the exaggerated stem of the clit on the drawing. 'This part got cut a bit when I was a baby.'

The woman didn't flinch. She covered Barbra's hand with her own. L-O-V-E was inked on her knuckles in blurry block script.

'That's a crime,' the woman said.

'Well, I have no memory of it.'

Then, as if unburdened, Barbra quickly checked off all the boxes. I slapped down my wallet on the counter exaggeratedly.

'We'll take a look, hon, okay? We'll see what we can do.'

Barbra palmed my wallet and extracted the card. The woman came out from behind the counter, shaking a pair of green plastic gloves.

'Lemme just talk to her for a second,' I said, throat closing. 'You can't do this.'

'I can,' Barbra said.

She gave me back my wallet. Then she followed the bald woman across the black-and-white-checkered floor. They both disappeared behind a hospital room divider. I shuffled forward like a roach.

Barbra was taking off her pants. They were red harem pants with tiny white flowers: a rectangular insert, a voluminous crotch.

'Hon, sorry. Tell your boyfriend he has to wait for you outside.'

The woman had her back to me. I wanted to tell her to fuck off. *She's* the one who should leave. The woman was searching inside some kind of medical cabinet. Barbra had settled into a white leather barber's chair. I slipped behind the curtain to scoop up her harem pants.

'Put these on,' I whispered. 'We just have to talk.'

Barbra did not look at me. I grasped the bone of her wrist.

'Did it hurt? Why'd they hurt you? Why did your family do that?'

Barbra smirked but she wouldn't look at me. I hadn't noticed anything about her vagina. I remembered that word on TV: *clitoridectemy*. I remembered the tears of Fatima and Tyra Banks crying *this beautiful woman just wants to be free.*

'Hon, come on. You have to tell your person to leave.'

'*No*,' I spat. 'Just give us a second.'

How did she bear all this hurt? I felt like my mother. Weak-kneed and soggy. Bubbles in my gut.

The lizard-eyed woman wielded a medical tray.

'This is *female* business.' She glared at me. 'This is your girlfriend taking back her power.'

Barbra finally looked me in the eyes. 'Not really. Sort of. Bruh, I'm *okay*.'

Then the woman put a headlight and reading glasses on. I stepped backwards. I walked backwards. But I could not leave.

'I'm just gonna look at what we got here, okay?'

Barbra nodded at the woman. She inched off her underwear. I thought, babies feel unconscionable pain.

'We're just going to take it nice and easy, okay?'

The woman used both her hands to gently part Barbra's legs.

'Slide toward me a little, hon.'

This woman approached Barbra's crotch, her plastic fingers in a V.

I smelled a gust of Windex. I stepped backwards a third time.

'I'm going to part your vulva now.'

I heard the front door of the shop open. The woman suddenly took off her glasses, upset.

'I can only do a small part on what's left of your hood,' she said. 'It might hurt a lot more because of your condition. I suggest labial, not clitoral today.'

The woman took off one plastic glove and caressed Barbra's feet.

'Let's *go*,' I hissed. '*C'mon*, just put on your pants!'

'This is your decision, hon.'

The lizard-eyed woman showed Barbra her tray lined with rods. Cotton balls, needle parts, a glimmering flint. Everything made me sick. This was permanent.

Barbra slid further downward in the chair and looked at me behind her.

'Go,' she said. '*Go*.'

Barbra picked a tiny ring from the row of little tools. The whole room vibrated. Someone was out there in the store poking through laminated pages. Labial and clitoral. The lizard-eyed woman dunked Barbra's ring into some aqua barbershop liquid. She was treating this like she was just shaving a head.

'You,' the woman said, 'are one very tough chick.'

I felt scissor-slice cramps. She was going to staple her vagina. I wanted to call my father. I was going to vomit or shit. Was piercing a part of her vagina seriously going to get her power back? Was that what my mother would have said?

I turned. I lurched past some man with white dreads. I see-sawed down the flight of stairs. I puked right in front of the jewellery store. People stepped away from me onto the street. Pinched clit. Foamy lizards. Clouds smothered the sun. I waited for Barbra at the jewellery store window where diamonds were lodged in filthy blue velvet hubs.

Barbra finally emerged from the doorway holding on to the woman. Her harem pants had a small patch of blood on one side.

'Hold on to her like I am,' the woman barked.

I caught Barbra right before she buckled on the sidewalk.

'She's got my numbers and a prescription. She says she wants wine.'

The woman squeezed Barbra's arm and went back upstairs. I took Barbra's full weight. She walked wide-legged, like a horse.

I felt helpless. We hobbled. Barbra could not see straight.

Then, halfway down the steps to the subway station, Barbra stopped and crouched.

'We can't stay here,' I said.

People stared and tried to manoeuvre around us. Barbra was shaking now, in a crouch, in a terrible sweat.

'We have to go either up or down.'

Barbra put her head on her knees. From halfway underground, I tried to field all the people. 'Give her space. Give space!'

Barbra kept shivering. I noticed the bleeding patch again. 'I'm calling my father.'

'No!' Barbra moaned. But she still didn't move.

I kept waiting and suggesting every few minutes that we move. This went on in the stairway for over an hour.

Finally, I called my dad at the hospital. I heard myself yelling at him in an echoing chamber.

'I don't want to be sent back,' Barbra cried one step above me.

She gripped my hand. I gripped back. 'That won't happen, I promise. He would never do that!'

Barbra was rocking back and forth. Wet hair. Sweat beads. Vaginal pain. I thought of the way that she sheltered the flame.

It took me and my father and a stranger behind us to eventually scale the stairway back out to the street.

We took her to the car, damaged and knock-kneed. She kept crying, 'That hurts, it hurts, stop it, please.'

My mother was gone. Now it was my job. I wanted to shelter her endlessly.

§

Time didn't move in the family room. Barbra passed Ariane the squat, man-faced pipe head.

'I wanna know what he's told you about me,' she said.

'Um, he said you were pivotal.' Ariane took a drag and passed the pipe back to Barbra. 'That you initiated him into the mysteries of perversity… And that *that's* why he loves being with women of colour.'

Barbra and Ariane suddenly exploded into laughter. Nostril smoke zigzagged like fireworks around them.

I thought, why do humans have to inexorably fuck? Why do they fuck with each other? They should just stop.

I knew I was anxious. Bornstein would've called it a fresh bout. I started deep breathing to help myself think. Barbra had her hand stuck to Ariane's flank. Breathing didn't work. How'd she know she liked that? I got more fucked up. I got very hard.

Do girls fuck other girls to bring buds to the trees?

I glanced at the shyster on a failed inhale. The shyster fucking creep-smiled at me. I heard sacrificial sounds. Sugarman had *excised* me. My neck pulsed in faint little pings on repeat. I refocused my dream. I excised this *creep*. I wanted Barbra to manoeuvre herself over *me*. I exhaled. Saliva in drops down my throat. Ariane's head tilted back on the edge of the couch. Her throat was all stretched out, serpentine. I shifted forward on my feet. She was submissive, unhinged. Double vision was addictive. Barbra's tongue was a barb. I felt cum in my balls. Snow fell. My sweat pooled. Barbra and Ariane tongue-kissing, tongue-fucking. I felt like a blob in the audience, spreading. Security men yanked me from Sugarman's lair. I squatted down. My dick was a rubber plant stem. Their stretched-open lips were one circle of fire. I had all this cum in me. Boiling, uprising. I knew Ariane's moans on repeat, on repeat.

Saliva was the juice of kissing. Saliva on waves slapping boats back and forth.

§

Maybe Joel had always had plans to infiltrate our relation. Joel sensed the sex stench, the bubble of me and Barbra together.

By Grade 10, Joel was doing GHB every single weekend because his tennis-club assholes had gotten him hooked. He had permanent pimples in a kind of star shape on his forehead. GHB made Joel even more intense about sex.

'Chicks like to just lie there and feel it,' he told me. 'They love to feel the fucking power of cock.'

Miriam still cooked and cleaned the house for his family, even though Joel's sisters had both basically moved out.

'You want the girls who receive the cock to think it's, like, fucking saving them or something.'

Miriam was still there every day when he was sixteen, making Joel's lunches and polishing the glasses.

'Dude, I gotta feel an ass twerk on my cock,' Joel said. 'One day, I swear, I'm gonna pay for it, fuck. Girls at our school, they don't know how to twerk.'

I'd only ever seen Joel's father a few times, the entire time that we were friends. He had this bushy brown moustache and was weirdly physically fit. I'd never seen a father who looked like him – dress pants, ballet-style pumas, and skin-tight white T-shirts without collars. He was a lawyer but he went to the office like that. Joel said that his father was a former world tennis champion.

'I want the ass at eye level. Twerk, bitch. Work it out.'

It made me really queasy the way Joel talked half the time. Like, since Barbra was here, he was watching porn with only

Black girls. He didn't know shit about Black girls. He was just chasing after me.

It occurred to me that Barbra was our final movement as friends.

By the middle of August, she was coming up to my room every night. Jew-boy and Suicide Girl, intertwined. My father went to work. We tried every bed in the house. She said, 'Bruh, tape my mouth.' I taped Barbra's mouth. I bound her hands with silver duct tape. She told me that I was the best Jew-boy abductor. The best Jew-boy wine buyer. The best Jew-boy with the best access to drugs.

'Do you believe in a punishing God?' Barbra had asked me.

'I believe in Joel,' I'd told her stupidly.

What I believed by the end of the summer was that I got punishment for the act of dehumanizing.

When we arrived at Joel's house, at first it seemed like Barbra just took it all in – Miriam singing in the kitchen, Miriam working at the sink, the spotlessness, the pot lights, the rows of wine bottles behind glass doors, five bathrooms for five people, everything. I had been stressed about Barbra meeting Miriam, but when it happened it didn't seem like a big deal at all. Miriam and Barbra just said hi to each other.

Then, later, in the basement, when we were all stoned, Barbra said out of nowhere: 'Middle-class folks: the fucking worst.'

Joel started laughing. 'Yeah, total hypocrites, man.'

'Middle-class folks gawk at the rich as if they think they're somehow different from them.'

I didn't understand what Barbra meant and the ways in which Joel had just seemingly agreed.

Joel packed another bowl up while Barbra turned to me.

'See, you're jealous of him. Your family's jealous of this. Class stratification's everything.'

Was this the same gruff Israeli way of seeing things?

Joel's basement was renovated, the exact opposite of ours where she slept. Class stratification? I was not jealous. I felt bad for Joel that his mother was never around. I thought his mother's absence maybe explained his alleged need for sexual conquest.

I realized that Joel was guffawing as I was thinking.

'What the fuck are you laughing at, man?'

'Because you looked fucked-up, bro! You look totally fucking shocked.'

'See, bruh, this family is at least upfront about its wealth,' Barbra said, as if I were a tool. 'They are not pretending to be middle-class, deceiving everyone.'

Deceiving everyone about *what*?

Now Joel was laughing so hard he almost could not speak. 'Yeah, but you should see it, though. His mom's into class war!'

'Shut the fuck up. Don't talk about my mother.'

After the clit pierce – Barbra had lied to my father and said it was her belly button – my father said I could not hang out with Barbra so much. He had to put her on antibiotics because she'd had a 101-degree fever two nights in a row.

My father thought Barbra should get her own friends.

My mother had believed in and nursed Barbra's trauma.

My parents, united, had not recognized in Barbra a growing, intractable need for transgression. They did not feel it, intractably, the way that I did.

The best way to imitate God, I'd read on sabbatean.com after the clit pierce, *is to cross every line, mix the sacred and profane.*

Joel smoked down the rest of the joint as he rifled through a few baggies of white powder. He poured out and corralled the powder into nickel-sized lumps. I wondered if she knew when she was technically crossing a boundary. Like, what if I left her to fend for herself here in Joel's pot-lit pit?

'She seems to get into more trouble with you,' my father said.

'I think I might just go home now,' I said.

I'd tried GHB once, not snorting, in a capsule. A few seconds after I'd washed it down with Coke, my tongue got so dry that I forgot how to talk. I remember coughing from that dryness like I was going to shoot out a lung. My cock didn't feel good. It didn't even get hard. I remember Joel told me to drink water, so I tried to drink water – he had one of those automated upside-down water machines – but I gulped it too quickly and it made a bubble in my stomach. It felt like a tiny piece of dung.

'Date-rape drug,' I said to Barbra as Joel portioned out powder to sell to his UCC friends. 'People choke on their own tongues. They vomit in their sleep.'

'We're not going to sleep.' Barbra smiled at me.

After my GHB night, I remember I woke up in the morning with my face covered in chunks. It took me a second before I realized that the chunks came from me. I was a sour-faced clown who'd skirted death in his sleep.

'Thing with G,' Joel said, changing the channel, 'is that your cock grows twice its size.'

'Total lie,' I said to Barbra.

'I got no cock,' she smirked. '*Yet.*'

God, I felt powerless to stop this inevitability.

Joel had a file of porn that he accessed on his forty-inch screen. For some reason, all the dudes he watched were hairy, tanned men. I stared now at one of his bears basically doing squats on top of the heads of two sorority-style girls in white lingerie. The guy bounced up and down like he was in the gym. The girls looked like mummified corpses underneath him with their arms crossed and tongues sticking stiffly straight up. That guy was trying to stake his asshole right onto their tongues.

'Truly fucking disgusting. This is like a horror movie,' I said. 'Like, a director actually *told* those girls to do that.'

'It's a job,' Barbra said. 'Those girls are getting paid.'

'Don't even listen to him, Barbra-girl. My G is premiere. You spew buckets of cum and wake up feeling fucking refreshed!'

God, I *hated* Joel in front of Barbra. I hated them together. I hated how they pretended to like the same things.

'You know, some freaks even plug it.'

'Plug it?'

'Up the anus, babe.'

Onscreen, the tanned bear kept bouncing on upturned dart tongues. Finally, he started splooging from all sides.

'I dare you, girlfriend! Look, I got this syringe.'

I watched one girl-mummy onscreen trade cum with the other, their spit strands stretching and fluctuating.

'This is not horror,' Barbra said. 'No one is dying, no one's dead.'

Wielding a dental syringe with a hummingbird beak, Joel poured one mound of G into a mug filled with water. He mixed it with a swizzle stick. Then, carefully lifting the plunger, Joel filled up the whole thing.

'Voila. Start with this.'

Joel handed the syringe upside down to Barbra. Then he started snorting stray powder and licking it off his upper lip.

'Go with her, you pussy-whipped mofo,' Joel said, sniffing.

God, Joel, when are you going to quit? Did his parents not care that he was a veritable drug addict? I did not think you could just quit hard drugs cold turkey. And *mofo*, to me, was a Sabbatian thing. Like, drugs in the anus would be God's way of *tsimtsumming*. *Tsimtsum*, I'd just read in an article by this Jewish UFO researcher, meant retreating, withdrawing – as in, turning down the volume on your speakers.

You have to *tsimtsum* to hear God at all, the guy said.

'Look, dude, if you hurry,' Joel said, switching the channel to hockey, 'we'll all be peaking exactly the same.'

I heard Barbra from the basement bathroom calling my name. I wanted to know her original name.

My mother had said Barbra needed space to be contrary. My mother thought that, for her whole life, Barbra had played by the rules. 'These rules were bigger than her when she was a girl,' my mother said. 'She was transplanted, adopted, forced to adapt. And now she needs to break the rules,' my mother said. 'This is instinctual and understandable and *normal*, okay?'

'Sounds like a bunch of social work BS,' my father said.

'Barbra was not able to finish the army due to trauma, that is explicit, that is written, and you know that,' my mother said.

Not quite, Mom, I wanted to interject. Barbra's a refusenik. The first Beta Israel refusenik. I wanted to put those words on a T-shirt. I wanted it to be public. I wanted her to be studied, respected. I wanted Barbra to feel proud of what she'd done.

'I heard that they put refuseniks in prison,' I said to her. 'Did you go to prison?'

'No, bruh. I came here,' Barbra offhandedly said.

I found her weirdly gleeful in Joel's fancy basement powder room. Just like my mother, liquefied glee.

'It's good I'm wearing this tonight,' she said.

Barbra was in a tube dress, all wrinkled, the colour of beet. I sat on the toilet. She got down on her knees. *Tsimtsum,* I'd learned, was the first contraction of God. A retraction so that the world could come into being. Barbra wiggled up her dress. I gawked at her panties. I thought, anuses contract. There are innumerable pleasurable nerve endings in the bottom, I remember our high school gym sex-ed teacher said.

I want to fuck you, I thought. *Just regular fuck.*

Our whole class erupted in hysterical laughter. Joel told me our gym teacher was definitely gay.

Barbra handed me the hummingbird syringe.

I wanted to rip down her panties. Touch her wayward clit ring.

God, let's leave the rich house, I thought. *Let the rich sing!*

Barbra contorted herself in the space between me and the toilet. She pulled her panties to one side.

'Do it,' she said.

I was staring. She wiggled. This was totally real. Stray black hairs. Volume rising. A tightening *tsim.*

'Come on,' she ordered.

'Nuh-uh.'

'Do it. I mean it.'

'I don't want to,' I said.

'I'll get *him* to do it then.'

Fuck. The hummingbird beak and the featureless face. I knew this would come back to haunt me, this cloudy piece filled with drugs. Barbra reached behind her, both hands, and spread herself open. I squinted at her asshole. A plunger. I plunged it inside.

'Come on, guys, I'm waiting!' Joel yelled from the playroom.

Barbra started laughing. She stood up, half-crooked, hand over her mouth. The beak fell on the floor. I knew I shouldn't have done that. I helped her *again* to step over the line. I burned on the john, both my hands in one fist.

'*Whoa.*' Barbra smiled at me. 'Hang on. Hang right on.'

Her dress was still up. She did not pull it down.

'My feet are stuck to the tiles,' she laughed.

Didn't it take longer than a second to kick in?

Barbra smiled down at me. I reached for her waist. I wanted to bring all of her to my face. I strung both arms around her and linked up my thumbs. I heard Barbra laughing, 'Move, feet, move on.' Her belly smashed into me. I should not have done that. She lifted her leg. She stomped her foot onto the lid of the toilet. Split legs. She opened. I got a gust in close-up. It was everything I wanted, a flash of bright light. Her ring was a third tooth, the bell hit my nose. I stuck out my tongue and she let me lick her. Descending from sky, perfect height for my face. My tongue up her pussy, slipperiness. I thought of my mother's last meal at home. Flickering candles. Pussy sea salt. Tears of white wax. Barbra's five-petal cunt rubbed itself on my tongue, on my nose. I touched the ring, retracted folds in this airless opening.

My father cried at the kitchen table immediately after my mom and Abigail left. His face grimaced, cheeks tight, as if he were reeling in pain. 'She's going to come back,' he kept saying. 'Your mother's going to change her mind.'

'Peakin', motherfuckers!' Joel's voice cut through the static.

Barbra sluiced off me too quickly and wiped her thighs clean. I felt like those girls in the porno flat on their backs – doing nothing, tongues stiff, just waiting. Barbra pulled her dress down and staggered out, leaving me.

I stayed in the powder room. All I'd needed was more time. I felt like a lump sitting on the lid of the john. I wanted to be her full pussy-licker, her disciple, her *bruh*. I wanted to learn Ge'ez, worship the Lion of Judah. I'd be the white Rasta man with the righteous Black wife.

The hummingbird beak rolled under the sink.

Standing in front of me: weighted feet, perfect height.

The real crime is when the helpers don't help.

With my pussy-slick face, I thought about Gregor Samsa. When Gregor was a bug, did he want everyone to be bugs? Did he want to turn his own sister into a bug?

And all those messianic Jews who followed an unstable liar, scuttling. I was thinking, do bugs, in fact, take care of other living things?

Maybe, I don't know, maybe I should not have been surprised.

In the playroom, Joel's cock was out over her head. Barbra half sat there awkwardly, leaning back on straight arms. It's true, his little purple dick had grown twice its size.

'You okay with it, bro?'

Barbra crawled away from Joel on her hands and knees. Then she lay on the floor right under the TV.

'My pussy's so wet, bruh. Feels like a frog.'

Barbra's dress was up, she was laughing and rolling side to side on her stomach. The lights had been dimmed but I saw Joel had put on a condom. He shuffled backwards now, hands up, and tripped on his jeans.

'Nothing happened, bro. Condom's dry. Check it. Fuck, dude. Come on. Don't look at me like that.'

My father missed my mother. I would miss Abigail like a centipede.

'Heart's racing, Jew-boy,' Barbra said to the floor.

'I didn't bang your girlfriend. Relax. Just change the channel, Jew-boy.'

'Fuck off,' I said. 'Don't ever fucking call me that.'

I watched Barbra try to roll over. She kept trying to push up off the floor as if she did not remember her arms. Do frogs have arms? Do bugs help each other? I thought for a second she was going to suffocate like that.

'It's wet. Is it blood?' Barbra slurred.

I went over to her. I crouched down hear her face. Face to the floor, she was total dead weight. She'd stopped moving. She seemed asleep. This was the end of the summer. All over her skin was this mossy, whitish sheen. Then Barbra started to twitch and her head cranked to one side. I was trying to lift her when she started vomiting.

'Joel, help me, fuck!'

I looked backwards. Joel was there, on the couch, half-slumped with his condom still on.

'Fucking wake up, man!' I screamed.

Barbra vomited again. The slew shot out in a throat-sized line.

'God, fuck, help me! *Do* something!'

She would not stop puking. Under the low-level pot lights, I sensed Joel trying to respond.

He slurred, 'Miriam. S'not awake for this, s'ry, s'my phone.'

Barbra's eyelids flickered, the colour of ash. I realized all of a sudden that there was shit underneath her. It came from her limbs, up her dress, all smeared underneath.

'Get up,' I hissed at her. 'You have to get up.'

Joel nodded off again. Another spasm of vomit. I found myself sweeping the table for his fancy drug phone. A puff of bad powder. I scrolled, fingers shaking, I scrolled around looking for Miriam.

'It's not working! She's not there!'

Joel was passed out. I kept pounding the screen. I saw the headline already: *Ethiopian-Israeli Exchange Student ODs*. She was breathing, but barely. Not aware of vomit nor shit.

'What's it, *boy*?' I heard Miriam's voice through the phone at full volume.

'She's unconscious!' I yelled. 'We need you. I don't know what to do!'

'Damn it to hell, man,' Miriam said.

I put my hand on Barbra's beet-coloured back. I fucking prayed she had enough air through her throat to come through.

Miriam finally arrived in the basement. Joel slept, drooling foam, with his pants still half-down. Miriam covered her nose. She saw the whole thing at once.

'What the fuck you two give this girl, then?'

Miriam marched up to Joel and slapped him hard on the head.

Joel roused, brow furrowed. 'G, man. Don't hit me,' he said.

Then Miriam crouched down beside me and touched Barbra's forehead. She forced open her eye, lightly palm-slapped her face.

'Look what you did to her. Just look what you did.'

'She's breathing,' I whispered. 'I made sure she was breathing.'

'What else you make sure of?'

'Should I have called the ambulance instead?'

'Check your head, man. You as brainless as he?'

My ears started ringing.

'Help,' Miriam ordered as she prodded Barbra's waist. 'Help me.'

I was confused for a second. Miriam had started wedging one hand under Barbra's waist and one under her left shoulder to try to roll her over. Miriam needed me to do the vomit-caked side. I stepped in her puddle. We tried to coordinate the flip.

'*You* don't be stupid no more,' Miriam said. 'From him, I expect.'

With my back propped up by the wall and my hand under Barbra's right shoulder, the two of us got Barbra on to her back. I would not be stupid. Her lips looked like seaweed. Miriam pulled a bunch of pillows from the couch and propped Barbra up diagonally.

'Go get a hot towel, man. Clean this smear face.'

Miriam cradled Barbra while she drilled an elbow into her stomach. I heard something gurgle, then rip.

'Go!' Miriam yelled at me.

She knew I was watching. I promised not to be stupid. Thank God, Barbra started coughing, then crying. She rubbed her mouth back and forth with her fist. I saw Barbra try to settle into Miriam's flowered armpit. Thank God, I prayed.

Buruk New, Ameyn.

§

'Why'd you come back here?' I asked her.

'I wanted to say sorry.'

I shook my head. My neck felt like a crooked stack of books.

'Bruh, why don't you believe me? I'm back to make amends.'

I'd joined her in the L-joint of the couch. I'd slithered over to her slowly. I knew she was impressed by my curated piles of books. I knew that she was looking for *her* book in there. Jim's store had closed years ago but I'd gone back one more time. I evacuated his Jewish Studies stock. He wouldn't even look at me. I wouldn't look at him either. Ariane and Barbra had somehow finished kissing. Stacks of books and piles of books. The shyster had pumped them full of his drugs. Ariane was now sleeping, her head near the shyster. I did not want to hurt her. I thought I had already betrayed her. Without my consent, this was happening again.

'Look, I'm telling you,' Barbra whispered. 'And I needed to do it in person. I am sorry for what I did.'

Seven years sloughed off from a part of my brain.

'I didn't mean to hurt you, just scare you,' Barbra explained.

I felt myself growing into some kind of fungus beside her. She was the main tree; I was mushrooming.

'If you forgive me,' Barbra whispered, 'we'll start up again.'

Seven years ago, I had to remove that book from my room as if it were a tumour from her body in my mind.

'Come on,' Barbra said. 'I'm not the same person.'

I'd climbed over the gate of the concrete lot of the building for victims of domestic abuse. The place had been slated for demolition.

I burned her sacred, stupid book with a whole pack of matches.

'It *means* something, bruh, if you *say* that you forgive me.'

I thought about my future. I thought about my mother. I thought about my hours of therapy undone.

My neck pulsed just like I always remembered it pulsing.

'Tell me your real name.'

Barbra leaned toward me, lips parted. She whispered a twisting, red invocation.

Then the ceiling cracked open.

'I forgive you,' I whispered.

For the first time in years I felt full of relief.

§

She'd said, 'Bruh, tape my mouth.'

She'd said, 'Bruh, light a match.'

Barbra kept egging me on. The last week of August. The dead, over-air-conditioned middle of the night. I didn't know why her lips had to be taped, why her hands had to be tied. It was like this invitation for me to do what I wanted, to think what I wanted, for me to feel power, for her to trust me with that.

But if I pictured her in Israel like this, she looked beaten, all curled up on some filthy street corner. I saw her bleeding and shaking, being taken away. This five-year-old girl all alone in a crowd. Baby girl held down and cut. Was her childhood an endless succession of traumas?

I thought Barbra invented the game of abduction to heal abduction.

And my mother had the nerve to say to me right before she left: 'You really need to take a break. I'm worried about your health.'

One night, Barbra said, 'I want something sharp.'

'Take a break,' intoned my mother. 'You and her should take a break.'

My mother didn't know what she was talking about. I thought my mother was getting in the way of her healing.

Barbra suggested scissors or a nail file. From my pencil case, I retrieved an X-acto blade.

Each night of August, toward the end, escalated.

'I'm not going to do anything crazy with this,' I said.

'*Crazy* is just one word out of many,' Barbra said.

I pretended to wield the thing like a weapon. I hammed it up for her, acting evil. I even licked the itty-bitty triangular blade.

'Stay away from her for a few days,' my mother pleaded with me from Portland. 'Doesn't Joel have a cottage? Can't you hang out with your friends?'

Shut up, I wanted to say to my mom. *You left. You just left. Now leave us both be.*

Barbra held her tits up, nipples right at her chin. I was an inextricable part of her performance of healing. Knives feel good, it was as if she was saying. Or maybe this was the title of the messianic healing performance: Knives Are Essential for the Jewish Sacrifice to Greet.

'Don't be scared,' Barbra said, looking up, her eyes drunk. 'Come on, hold it right over me.'

Why? Fuck. I didn't want to hurt her. I wanted to cut my own arm with her name.

But I walked up to her with this weapon she chose. Barbra looked up at me and stuck out her tongue. I shuffled in closer. Barbra knew what she was doing. I wanted to yell: *Are you sure? Are you sure?* Barbra pulled down my pants. I got weak. She inhaled. With the knife upraised in my right hand, Barbra opened her mouth wide, pulled me in and started sucking. I heard her saliva. I felt her lips clutch. Barbra slit her eyes, staring upward, engorged with me.

I wobbled. She kept telling me what to do.

'Cut. God.'

My knife came down and grazed the top of her tit.

Abuse, that's abuse, my mother said.

Barbra went all the way. She gagged like a porn clip.

Sacrifice, I thought I heard myself say.

I smelled Windex perfume. I felt my pubic hairs itch.

'More,' Barbra gurgled. 'Do it again.'

She was doing this rub-and-squeeze thing with one hand at my balls. I let the blade nick the skin again at her tits. I felt like a killer. A ruby stud glistened.

'Again,' she ordered, not taking a break.

I heard myself moaning, pathetic. I did not want to hurt her. Why was she putting me in this position? I felt like a bad man enacting bad things. I felt like the hairy-ass bear in Joel's porn, the one who didn't care that he face-fucked girls playing dead.

'I don't want to,' I moaned. 'Let me out of this script.'

Barbra sucked the head of my bright pink cock back into her redness. She tugged from the root. I stared down at her nipples. I hated my total obeisance.

'Let's stop,' I pleaded.

Barbra shook her head no.

'Are you going to stay with us all year?' I whispered, weak-kneed, still holding the blade. 'Are you going to go to college here like my dad said?'

'If you promise me you're up for it.' Barbra wiped the corners of her mouth of saliva.

'What's "it"?' I moaned.

'Your undoing.'

I felt just about to cum. Her tit had marks on it – notches in a half-circle, like a sun dial. My chest burned. *I'd* done that. What was my undoing? Pushing Barbra off me? Making her lie on her back? Making her spread her legs just a little so I could see that studded bump under her panties, all her undulating.

'Yeah, I like that,' she said. 'Stand right over me.'

She lay on her back and stared at the knife in my hand. I straddled her waist.

'Pretend now,' she said, 'that you're gonna murder me.'

I lurched. 'No! Fuck. I would *never* do that.'

'Stop saying *no*. Keep using that thing.'

'I don't want to. I don't have to.'

'But you're stopping me from feeling.'

'Feeling *what*?'

Isaac and Abraham. Female victimhood. The sparks of God all over this room.

'Jew-boy, I'm telling you, you can slice up these panties.'

The knife slipped in my grip. 'But why, tell me *why*.'

I felt sweat roll down the sides of my face. I crouched over her. I did not want to 'slice up these panties.' I did not want to undo. I did not want to sin. I wanted to go to the beach. Hold her hand. Fuck. But I pretended to draw a line down her belly with the paper cutter, the triangular blade. Barbra quivered. She said *yes*. I went lower. She said *yes*. I pulled out the elastic waist of her panties. She was breathing so fast. Freezer burn hit my eyeballs. I sliced the elastic. It snapped. The panties of Barbra. I was afraid that she was going to be afraid. I slit down the fabric thinking I was a killer. I ripped the fabric thinking: human beings *stab* human beings. But my cock pulsed so hard that it beat in my neck. I was right at her pussy. I kept slicing down. All her hair in a flame. I split up her panties. I put one finger right at her lips where they opened. I felt a gush of excess. Her clitoris. Her undoing. I wanted to suck it. Was this what she wanted? She kept saying *yes*. I felt water roiling. Her cunt skin was shiny, crowned with a clit bell. I pushed up to my knuckle. I felt saucer knees. She bucked up to my palm. Prickly hairs on my wrist. I slid one more in. Two fingers hooked. Her whole cunt squeezed my fingers. Circle bone, mushy trap.

She moaned at me, 'Use that little knife thing.'

My fingers were full-on fucking her now, no longer truly attached to my brain. I felt her cunt, her whole body, gnaw up through my surface. *Get the condoms, Jew-boy*, my mother would've said. I kept rearranging myself. I held my cock for a second. This did not seem real. I could not get things in sync. My bobbing red cock felt like a part of some other body, a greater machine. My brain was outside me. Would she accept me? Why did I still hold the ritual knife? I was pulled by sensation. I slid my cock in her. Her bell touched my base. *God, finally.*

'Don't move, just stay still,' Barbra said.

She closed her eyes. She breathed hard.

I did what she said. I lay in a tableau. Her pussy got really hot. It ballooned on my cock. Like it was gorging, regorging, coming out of itself. I was going to cum inside with no condom.

Don't you dare, my mom said.

Go on, Jew-boy, come.

My eyes rolled. Dropped the knife. Ripped panties. Black tape.

God, I backslid. My cum pooled on the floor underneath our four legs. She rolled away from me blind. I watched her slick naked. She crawled on all fours. Her ass started shaking. She wasn't really moving, just her ass was. A bouncing, blurry, butterflied sponge. She put her fingers inside herself. I saw this weird shining circuit of pinkish white light. Squelching sounds came. She was butterfly-fucking. Gnawing on air, bouncing her ass. I got instantly hard all over again. I looked back and forth between her ass and her pussy. There I was, fire rod, bucking in time. I watched her ass shake till she fucked something out of her. I watched her ass shake till her cunt squirted a spring.

§

In the rotunda, the forces of security were hiding. Professor Sugarman told me that I could not call my thesis *The Hoax of Early Holocaust Lit.* Fine. This was it. Our final showdown. Sugarman was forty years old, pregnant with twins. She admitted to me that her brain had gone lax. I told her that I would think of a more specific pronouncement.

I came up with *The Goat Humper and the Schizophrenic.*

'Your work is important, don't cheapen it,' Ariane said.

'You are joking, surely,' Sugarman said.

No. *The Goat Humper and the Schizophrenic* might win a Pulitzer Prize!

In fact, *goat humper* came straight from this text I read by Sander Gilman about Jewish bestial proclivities – this was back when people told anti-Semitic stories to rouse each other to pogrom, when it was rumoured that Jewish women fucked goats because their weak-dicked men were busy sex-murdering Christians.

I said to both Sugarman and Ariane at different points, 'Guys, free association is not mind-cheapening!'

Ariane knew I couldn't make the institution work. She knew I was not a born academic like her. Ariane was writing about the unpublished works of Iris Chang. *Everyone* wanted Ariane's stuff. She got every single scholarship she'd ever applied for. Just like Abigail, it occurred to me.

After two straight years under Sugarman and Ariane, what I'd come up with for my thesis was this:

1. Truth is subjective.
2. Sadism is pervasive.
3. Victimhood is not a permanent state.

I shut out weird thoughts of Barbra molesting my mind as I walked through the rotunda for the seven-thousandth time. I got very specific. This was my thesis. She could take it or leave it. I went to Sugarman's office, banging on her door.

'After World War II, listen to me,' I said, 'the men and the women who had been concentration camp inmates needed to tell the world what had happened to them, right?'

'Right, right,' Sugarman absentmindedly said.

'And sometimes, they embellished, sometimes they spun high-octane yarns. Sometimes they even took shits on the page! I do not want to call this testimony! I want to call this literature. Political literature. Not diversity.

'Sugarman, listen. This is my A-B-C-D:

The traumatized prevaricate.

To hoax is to live in the state of survival.

Survivors aren't empty, they're frenzied.

Language is perverse.'

'These are not my scheduled office hours,' Sugarman said.

'Dr. Sugarman, just hear me out, please! *The Hoax of Early Holocaust Lit*, also known as *The Goat Humper and the Schizophrenic*, is based on the most important book of Holocaust fiction, the first-ever book of Holocaust fiction. *House of Dolls* by Ka-Tzetnik 135633. Sugarman, you asked me what is my thesis *really* about? It's about a half-naked, blond, cleavage-ridden death-camp prostitute! Separated from her mother and brother, Daniela was forced to service German soldiers at Auschwitz. And Harry, the narrator of *House of Dolls*, details his sister's victimhood as if he were watching. That's an important part: *as if he were watching.'*

Sugarman sighed. She gulped Gatorade, gripped her phone.

'*House of Dolls*,' I continued, 'made Ka-Tzetnik famous, right? In the sixties and seventies, *House of Dolls* was taught in every Israeli school *as fact. House of Dolls* sold over five million copies. It was studied and read as the worst-case scenario, i.e., the ultimate degradation: the sexual exploitation of the teenaged, blond Euro Jew.'

'You know that that book has been discounted as pornography,' Sugarman said.

'Yes, and I also know that we have enough brains to understand the polymorphous ways people process suffering!' I screamed.

'You look skinny, you look tired. Are you sure that you're eating? Taking your meds?' Sugarman stared at me, unmoved.

'Look,' I said, shaking, trying to compose myself, convince her. 'According to the Holocaust scholars, you are right, yes, Ka-Tzetnik 135633's *House of Dolls* is not "true" – and it definitely is not based on any teen prostitute's diary. *House of Dolls*, according to the Holocaust scholars, is nothing more than overwritten kitsch. Holocaust scholars, you're right, are all in agreement: there were no Jewish whores at Auschwitz. Holocaust scholars remind us that, according to the law at that time, German men weren't even allowed to have sex with Jewish women. The Joy Division at Ravensbrück, for example, was staffed with former Communists and Polish sex workers.'

'Okay, good, so we're sort of on the same page,' Sugarman said.

'But what I will put forth in *The Goat Humper and the Schiz-ophrenic* is that it does not really matter if there were literal Jewish whores at Auschwitz because traumatized people like Ka-Tzetnik *tell the truth*. In order to confess, one has to lie, Kafka said.'

'Can't you feel you're stepping into quicksand?'

'No.'

Sugarman pounded her fist on her desk. 'This should not be your focus. Why is this your focus? Focus on the text. Leave and don't come back until you can focus on the proper *meaning* of the narrative.'

In Ka-Tzetnik's *House of Dolls*, survival meant trickery and sexual pain. Daniela was sterilized. Barbra flashed through my head.

'You can't just breeze over the most formative experience of the man's life,' Sugarman said. 'You have to tell us how Ka-Tzetnik's suffering at Auschwitz made him a writer. He wrote all those books *about* Auschwitz, right? He wrote about female suffering and sexual subjugation. What did this *do* to his language? What does this all *mean*?'

It means that, yes, female sexual subjugation was real but sometimes it was *also* a mirage – like in pornography! Come on, doctor, look at some porn!

I took a deep breath. I felt like I was losing this thing.

'Ka-Tzetnik 135633 is actually more like a pornographer than any kind of documentarian,' I said to Sugarman, doing my best imitation of a rising academic star. I had to forcefully clip Barbra's spread-open cunt lips and cunt bell out of my head.

Sugarman bristled.

'And so, uh, his pornographic slant is what makes his work coded and feminist, meaning important to explore.

Coded and feminist transgression,' I insisted, 'is not a lie. It should not be rejected. I don't care if we're talking about Auschwitz, all right?'

'Ka-Tzetnik is a *survivor*,' Sugarman said. 'That's fact. And if you're going to focus on his work, you have to understand that the texts of Ka-Tzetnik 135633 are essentially texts of *witness* and *survival*. Non-fiction, auto-fiction, science fiction – call it what you want, I don't care. But if you don't show me that you have understood *multivalent critical theories* on Holocaust literature, then I cannot be convinced that you understand your own starting point.'

'*House of Dolls* is my starting point! Pulp, porn, lies: the fist of art. It's phantasm. She-wolves. This woman inside my basement. There were no Jewish whores in Auschwitz, fine, but there was racism, sexism, buckets of jism…'

Sugarman spilled bright yellow Gatorade all over her papers.

Ka-Tzetnik wrote books to try to release his suffering. Barbra drank wine to release her suffering. She followed me around our house with a knife.

'I think you should leave now,' Sugarman said.

'Trauma's a branch of pornography, doctor! It's the release of suffering from the lab of suffering!'

I heard Barbra's dithering moans. I smelled her vomit again. I wanted to tell the whole world that I was not like Joel and all those other numbskull porn fans: in porn is latent joy, full-blown *suffering*.

'Sugarman, human beings need pornography to work out their trauma,' I kept going. 'This aspect of Ka-Tzetnik's work was not supposed to be misunderstood!'

'I think we've talked enough about your project for today,' Sugarman said, standing up behind her desk with her phone.

Sugarman's husband emerged in my mind as some taxman-type cog squirming around at his desk. Dude shot her up with multiple sperm.

I stood my ground and forced Sugarman to keep listening to me. 'When the ragged survivor who renamed himself Karl Tzetnisky arrived in Palestine armed with his first novel,' I said, 'he changed his name to Yehiel Dinur. Dinur was sprayed with DDT at a holding camp. His head was measured. He was fingerprinted.'

'DDT? Where are you getting this? *Stop.*'

'*De-nur* means "of the fire" in Aramaic,' I continued. 'But Ka-Tzetnik did not rise in Palestine triumphant – he slithered and hid in his suffering.'

Sugarman handed me the dregs of her Gatorade. 'Have a drink. Please. You look ill,' she said.

Barbra, the leghold trap in our basement, slithered in while I was gulping.

'You need to at the very least read Ruth Franklin,' Sugarman said, still holding her phone like a weapon. 'Which, as it happens, I've been telling you to do for a year. *A Thousand Darknesses* is a masterwork. It speaks *exactly* to what you are working on, truth and variation, the burdens of truth, truth and the context behind what we call lies.'

I realized that the doctor had not been listening to me.

'Because what I want to know, actually, what *offends* me,' Sugarman continued, 'is why you want to act like no one before you has ever thought of this stuff? Because this is how we work here: we rely on reading each other's texts. We read each other as Jewish thinkers in order to work on our own thoughts and build other, newer things.'

But that was not how I wanted to work. I wanted to make

completely new readings of every single Jewish thing. Ka-Tzetnik's proximity to truth was truth enough for me. Truth was an in-and-out slithering.

'Does your husband like it when you get all worked up?' I asked Sugarman, laughing.

'Okay. That's it. I'm calling security. This is over. We are done here,' Sugarman said.

§

Ice coated the telephone wires. My father's Benz was buried under wedges of snow. I rammed my spine into the wall underneath my window ledge. My father had usually left for the hospital by now.

Ariane appeared in the doorway fully dressed. She walked in and sat on the edge of my bed.

'What's wrong?' she said.

I yanked her by the arm. Barbra behind my eyelids at the edge of a cliff.

'Stop,' she said.

But I'd already got her off balance. Now I just had to wrestle her in. I got her under the covers. I started biting her neck.

'They're all awake down there. Stop it. Come on, your dad, too.'

Ariane smelled like smoke from last night. I wanted to fight her. I felt like a bat. I had to tell her and my father where I was going. I unbuttoned her pants. Ariane started struggling. How long had I been sleeping? I felt my blood rushing.

'Stop. Come downstairs with me,' Ariane said.

But I manoeuvred myself on top of her and pulled her jeans down to her calves.

Barbra didn't want the shyster anymore. She told me her real name. She wanted *me*.

I started licking two-tongued down Ariane's stomach, keeping her plastered down on my bed. I swished into her belly button and she started to squirm. I remembered her tongue last night filling Barbra's mouth.

'Come on, stop. Let's go downstairs.'

Jew-boy, that was an hallucination.

I dragged my tongue swishing through Ariane's pubic hairs. I gripped her thighs. I knew exactly what she liked. I squeezed Ariane's ass cheeks from underneath and I split them. She rocked into me. This would be her goodbye. Ariane loved being opened from behind. Why were they kissing? I did not make this up, I still heard the saliva. I forced Ariane all the way up and down the length of my face. Her pussy tasted icy. My nose was all coated. In the upstroke I found suction on Ariane's clit. Her clit was like a stone underwater. It turned oily when I sucked it. I plunged my first finger up into her from behind. I did two. I found her asshole with my pinky. Ariane gripped my whole head with her thighs and she pumped.

I couldn't get my words out.

I'm going back to Israel.

Ariane stopped and pulled me up.

'What?' I said.

'*Nothing.*'

'Come on, why'd you stop it?'

Ariane with flushed cheeks rolled out of my bed. 'Because I'm just not feeling it right now.'

I was going to have to break up with Ariane.

For the last few months, she'd been trying too hard to get in my head. She'd even started doing research for me, trying to work her academic magic. I was almost ready to break up with Ariane.

'Germany is now open to excavation of its past,' Ariane told me, reading some website on her phone about an exhibit in Berlin on the brothels in concentration camps.

'So even if he was fantasizing,' Ariane continued, 'your guy was actually there!'

I hated how she called Ka-Tzetnik 'my guy.'

'There were brothels in *ten* concentration camps,' Ariane read. 'Between three hundred and four hundred Jewish prisoners were forced to become sex workers. Okay, listen, it says here that a visit to a brothel, known as a "special barrack," was part of a system of incentives intended to boost the productivity of concentration-camp slave labourers.'

Ariane seemed so proud of herself. It was like she thought she'd found me the magic ticket, the ticket to our future togetherness, to everything.

'Do those Germ-boys admit that those places were basically pussy for the *Judenrat*?'

Ariane looked up at me, extremely disturbed.

'I mean, the complicit Jews. The rich Jews. The ones who tried to save their own skin.'

'Uh, babe, I get that you're not addressing the exploitation of women in your thesis,' Ariane said. 'Like, I totally understand that you're not looking at rape as a war crime, okay? But my point still stands that your guy Ka-Tzetnik was working from *reality* – I mean, *real* brothels, right? *Not* made-up brothels. That's all that I was trying to say.'

It bothered me that Ariane could find rape culture in everything. She was right, I was not dealing with rape as a war crime, but I wasn't trying to say that it didn't happen either.

'Ka-Tzetnik wrote pulp, but he was not a rape apologist,' I said.

'Yes, I understand that,' said Ariane.

'No, you don't.'

'Yes, I *do*. And I think whatever you do is going to be brilliant.'

'Stop lying. You do not.'

'Babe, what's wrong with you? I *told* you to apply to UC Berkeley and the European Grad School. They get your work.'

I laughed. I couldn't help it even though Ariane looked hurt.

'Come on, Ariane. You *know* that Berkeley is not going to take me – one hundred and fucking ten percent. And European Grad School lets in any fool with cash.'

'Why are you being so aggressive?'

'Let's just stop talking.'

'No. *Why*?'

'I don't want to talk about this anymore.'

'*Why*? I'm not saying anything wrong! I'm trying to support you. All I do, babe, is try to support you.'

I told Ariane that I didn't need support. I needed money. I needed to be published, to be taken *seriously*.

'But that's what I'm saying, babe. Come on, you *will* be!'

I felt like she was destroying me with support. It took everything in me not to just scream *shut up*. Ariane literally could not stop this kind of conversation once we'd started. She could never ever just leave things alone. She always had to be right. She even wanted to hug me. I did *not* want to hug her after talking like this.

But something about her rape comment stuck.

I thought, Ka-Tzetnik *did* experience rape as a war crime. Being in a concentration camp was like being raped. I thought,

Ka-Tzetnik left Auschwitz *primed to pervert*. I thought, feminized, traumatized men want to pervert the whole world! I thought about Sabbatai Zevi, Barbra's slippery Messiah. I thought, the salamander was a cold-blooded, slippery lizard. I thought, victims are perverts. God, I would never say that out loud. Ariane would've said I was brainwashed or racist. My father would've had me committed again.

But I knew that I would finish my thesis, school or no school. I would write this thought down: *Perversion is just a fantastic action committed by a hurt person that taps the heart of the world.*

'You *have* to introduce Ka-Tzetnik's pulp into the canon.' Ariane kept talking, trying to smooth over whatever was going on between us. 'Because most Jews seem to think they are exempt from being "bad."'

I started laughing out loud. What did she think being 'bad' had to do with being Jewish? Was she back on the essentialist, exploiting, bad-white-man thing?

This was a question for Barbra, I thought. Barbra pervert tapping.

'Stop laughing at me,' said Ariane.

I wanted to tap the whole world with my Beta Israel refusenik.

'*Israel bombs little kids.* We've all seen the videos,' Ariane said.

Feminized, traumatized men humped goats in my head.

'Stop looking at me like that!' cried Ariane. '*I know* that "Jew" does not equal Israel. I *know* that there's dissent inside of Israel. I *know* it's a steady war of propaganda between the master and Indigenous narratives.'

'You have no idea what you're talking about,' I said.

I felt ready to split. I felt primed to pervert. I could not look at my girlfriend anymore in the eyes.

'Wow, look here. White fragility, folks. Look here, it's *real*.'

Why did Ariane always think she knew what was right, what was real?

'Israel bombs little kids, babe. That's a *fact*. I know you can hear me. Operation Cast Lead. There is no defence.'

I had no more defences. Barbra had re-entered my basement. She'd cut through my barbed wire, sliced into my real.

§

My father's chest hairs formed the shape of a mushroom cloud. All the newspapers were open on the kitchen table.

'Stop crying, I'm not mad. C'mon, kid. Get up.'

Barbra was kneeling on the ground in front of my father's pyjamas. My dad touched her shaved head, glancing guiltily at me.

'We should tell Abigail and your mother – looky-look who's back.'

Barbra got up off the floor. She was *crying*. For *him*? Did she apologize to him like she'd apologized to me? Ariane somehow swooped in and linked arms with Barbra, leading her over to the stove.

My father displayed multiple, layered frown lines. 'You know, now I feel like I want a cigarette.'

Barbra lobbed a pack of Israeli cigarettes on the table.

'*Regga*, Barbra, *regga*. *Oy*, I mean, *b'vakesha!*'

Barbra giggled. What was happening? Was this comic relief? Where was the shyster? Plugging a bomb in the pipes? My dad fiddled with the package. He hadn't smoked since he was a student. I thought of Joel for some reason, back here as a dick-ish director: *Did your father fuck her, too, bro? Let's work with something here where this hot Black girl from Israel is like the mail-order bride and she's fucking both the father and the son with a hot Chinese lesbian lover on the side...*

My father extracted the lighter from Barbra's pack of cigarettes.

'*Oy! Slicha.* Barbra. I'm sorry. I'm rusty. It's been seven years.'

Why wasn't my father more fucking concerned about *me*? Why didn't he think about what this was doing to *me*?

Ariane and Barbra huddled together at the oven. My father was cross-eyed, lighting up.

'Don't you have to go to work today?' I asked him.

'Let's call your sister.'

'Why?'

My mother and Abigail would not want to know about this. They wouldn't want to know about the sordid scene last night either, shyster smoke, girlfriends intertwined. Abigail, especially, would be horrified. Nineteen years old, my sister was the only one of us who had totally cut out Barbra from her mind.

My father lobbed his phone at me. 'Check when the plows are coming through.'

Abigail said that she did not have time for liars. Liars disrupted her focus. She called Barbra a leech.

I was knee-deep in leeches. Leech-liars triggered my thinking, my cock getting hard.

The kettle shrieked. What the fuck were Barbra and Ariane *doing*? My father was watching the asses of my girlfriends. God, I needed to calm myself, stop the chaos: think.

'You making coffee there, Barbra? *A bisl chalav. Todah rabah.*'

'I need to talk to you,' I hissed at my father, who sucked on his first cigarette in thirty fucking years again and again.

'Just a sec,' said my father, proud of his Hebrew, trying to get Barbra's attention.

I hissed my truth. '*Now*.'

But everything felt too late. There was no time for *now*. It was too late for some kind of alignment with my father. I'd been trying too hard. I'd soaked up his methods of control. Like, my whole entire life I'd soaked in this brine. Like, the way he could talk himself out of anything – *anything* – by framing himself as the hero. My father's mock self-deprecation, bad smoke inside our kitchen. The way he talked to my mother, the way he talked to me.

'*Chalav* and *a bisl tsuker*. Like a latte, okay? Sugar's right there. I like a little latte.'

Like Kafka, I hated my father. Then the shyster walked in.

'Who's this?' said my father, genuinely surprised.

The shyster wore a matted red terry-cloth robe. His hair was all out, wiry white and down to his shoulders. He entered the kitchen to shake my father's hand.

I was riveted by my father's reaction, how he received the Frenchman as a threat to his kingdom. He refused the hand and popped up like a jack-in-the-box.

'You slept here? Barbra?' My father was suddenly hostile, completely confused.

'Dr. Christof Laliberté. I speak Hebrew and Amharic. A little Arabic, too.'

My father looked at me, his lips downturned. Involuntarily, I smiled. My father took a stress drag.

'I don't understand,' my father said. 'I'll be honest with you.'

'I do mediation,' said the shyster. 'My specialty.'

I laughed out loud. Cock fight! My father rushed at me, smoking. He gripped my T-shirt to yank me out of the kitchen with him. I saw Ariane looking at us over her shoulder. It was totally clear to me what Ariane was thinking: my father's aggression was mine, too, all mine.

My father huffed on his cigarette. 'They call that schmuck out there a *mediator*?'

His clown face was morphing, lips encircled with stubble.

Schmuck was better than *shyster*. My dad was always outperforming me.

'I can't believe that's who they sent.'

I stared at my father. 'You *knew* she was coming back here?'

'No, *no*. I didn't know. No, I didn't. Not like this.'

My father paced. I could not fucking believe this. I banged my forehead on the front door.

'Stop. Don't *do* that. It's not true. I didn't know. Stop. Come on. You're getting way too excited.'

I kept banging my head on the door. Ladies, can you hear? *This* is how I deal with my father's passive-aggression. Drum skull, numbskull.

'Stop it. Calm *down*!'

I decided not to stop. I wanted a horn on my forehead.

'Stop banging your head or I'm calling the cops.'

That seemed like a lie. The horn of abuse.

But it was the first time in a long time that me and my father had really looked at each other. Long hairs off his eyebrows acted like a thicket over his two purplish blood-vessel lids. My own eyes felt glazed. Our vision, vibrating.

'Why didn't you tell me she was coming back here?'

'Because I did not know that she was coming back here with a crazy person!'

'I thought I was the crazy person.'

My father took a last suck of his wrinkled cigarette, glancing backwards at the kitchen.

'It is our duty to forgive her,' he whispered.

I felt like dragging that spark through his mushroom-cloud tits.

'She called me a few times from rehabilitation. Okay, she called me two times, maybe more, maybe a few years ago.'

Bang. My father told lies.

'Jesus Christ! Stop! She called from South America some-where. I didn't think she would actually come back for real. We both know she's cuckoo, okay?'

The horn in me rising. *Cuckoo* and *schmuck*.

'I didn't tell you because I didn't want to upset you! Look at you,' my dad yelled. 'Calm yourself, please!'

I felt my head bump sprout into two distinct sections. One was reconciliation and one was rusted destruction.

I wanted to alter this story. Did my father not remember? I banged my forehead on the door one last time. My horn grew. My father put his hand on my shoulder. Then he started crying wetly and honking, just like clowns cry.

My father was full of denial, the falsest control. He'd brought Barbra here and now he'd brought her back.

'Where's my phone? You have my phone? Let me phone Bornstein.'

I started pacing in front of the dented-in door. My father, in fact, had orchestrated this.

'We're going to get you an appointment *today*.'

Snorting to breathe, protecting the door, I realized it was not my father's job to continue to take care of me. I realized that my father was afraid of my encroaching 'psychosis.' My father was afraid of cunt. Quitting school. Rekindling.

'I'm going to go with her to Israel,' I said.

'No, you're *not*,' my dad hissed, phone glued to his ear. 'Ariane's a good girl. The other one is cuckoo.'

I thought, *My horn will be psychic, sacrosanct strength.*

With short steps, my father turned in a circle. 'You can't leave right now. You need to finish that degree.'

My father didn't even know what the fuck I was writing about. His cigarette stuck like a bug on the floor. Sugarman had excommunicated me.

'It's not complicated,' my father said, turning in on himself. 'They said she just wanted to apologize to us. That's why she's here. It's not complicated. *Stop.*'

Spit brewed at the back of my throat. My father wanted Barbra back for his own fucking reasons.

'I'm going to Israel.' I said it again.

'Yeah, yeah, I have him right here.' My father was finally speaking to a person.

Dear Father: I am involved in perversion.

My father looked up at me. 'Bornstein has morning, tomorrow, for an emergency session.'

My head buzzed. My arms shook. All vibrations from her. This new-old space in our minds we would finally pierce through.

'Thank you. Thank you,' my father said. Then he hugged me too hard, drenched in a scary, tarry odour.

Outside, the snow fell in intertwined flakes.

Victimhood is not a permanent state.
In Israel, I thought, we'd resume our sex games.
Cuckoos pierce reality.

Future

S he came back for me the first Monday in March, the day that I quit school for good. She took me to Israel on cheap-flights.com two days later. My father alerted my mother and my sister. Ariane barraged me with texts.

You need to stay. Call out Sugarman. Finish things.

It was as if no one wanted to believe this was real. But I packed a real bag. I changed my cash to real US dollars. Ariane knew that my thesis had really been quashed.

I miss you, Ariane texted when I got through security in Toronto. *I'm crying all the fucking time.*

Yeah, Ariane missed my cunt-licking with crocodile tears.

My father got my mother on a conference call where both of them told me their side of the story, more of the story, trying to stop me from leaving. My father said that seven years ago, Barbra had been sent to rehab in Israel. My mother explained it as this kind of half-rehab, half-juvenile detention. It was in Dimona, specifically for kids of Ethiopian ancestry. My father added that he and my mother had signed some kind of legal agreement so that Barbra would not have to go to a real Israeli jail. My mother said that she'd found this program because she wanted Barbra to know that the diaspora, at least, was aware of Israel's problems with race.

'Barbra's *always* been aware,' I spit through the phone line at both of my parents, 'of Israel's fucking problem with race.'

Then my father told me that Barbra had received a full U of T Comparative Literature scholarship. My mother said it was a real pity that Barbra couldn't follow through on this.

'Jews need more voices of colour in our academic ranks,' my mother said.

'Your mother continues to set up this false dichotomy banking on the fact that Jews are considered white. Jews aren't *white* people,' my father said.

'You're right. Jews are a multiple, racialized population.'

'Back to your old tricks, Ruth. Nothing has changed.'

'It's Jews like you who need to take lessons on race equality from Islam.'

I came to the conclusion before my return to Israel that both my mother and my father were were deluded, subjective, outmoded. And I know that they thought they'd done the right thing seven years ago when they agreed not to press charges against her.

But I had to get armed with my own conclusions.

I thought, family is bunk if one interloper can destroy it. Family is bunk if some stranger can root out the weak link.

I concluded: the interloper is the instigator. The interloper helps the weak link pierce through his wrong thinking.

And then, Mom and Dad, the weak link strikes back.

The weak link makes a choice.

The weak link is always going to lean toward the future.

The weak link does not subscribe to meek, clannish thinking.

The weak link won't play nice and conciliate.

Conciliation, Mom and Dad, is *charity*. Charity is the saviour fantasy.

*Re*conciliation, on the other hand, is hard fucking work – inner work – with *penalties*.

§

The schmuck drank five mini-bottles of vodka on the plane. Barbra guzzled wine. I used headphones, watched *Homeland*. My gut cramped up with chicken-breast gas.

In the middle of the flight, I awoke with the schmuck's claw on my flank.

'Would Leila Khaled like to blow up this plane?'

In the plane's dim abyss I got spooked and recoiled. I thought, what matters is that Leila Khaled did not kill anyone.

Going to Israel with that girl is highly dangerous, my mother messaged me before we boarded.

I unbuckled my seat belt and limped to the back of the plane.

My mother's second message lit up as soon as we landed: *Dangerous for your abusive dynamics.*

Since my mother had turned into a West Coast professor, she said that Indigenous peoples in this world bore the full brunt of violence *qua* structural inequality. My mother said that Palestinians were Indigenous and that we were the settlers with all the abuse and domination that colonization brings.

'Jewish people need to stand down,' my mother said. 'Right their wrongs. Clean shop. Take responsibility.'

'She makes no sense,' my father raged. 'What about *Arab* Jews? "Clean shop"? Gimme a break. And can your mother explain to me why the Moroccans are the most right-wing?'

'A society that colonizes has no conscience,' my mother responded. 'Military rule is the only way to keep a people amoral. It is the only way to make teenagers killing machines.'

'Killing machines? Jesus Christ, Ruth. What's in your soup? We need soldiers because it's *war*. It's war when you're *surrounded* by enemies. This is not rocket science. Israel is *communal*. Jews work together to make sure that we're safe. If you lock your door over there in Portland, that's called *security*, yes?'

'Israeli kids have nightmares,' my mother said. 'Palestinian kids lose their entire beds.'

'My God, what part of this equation don't you understand? The Jews are protecting themselves from *extermination*.'

'The ceiling erupts,' my mother continued. 'Kids with rubber bullet holes in their foreheads.'

'*Oy*, I am begging you,' my father lamented. 'Why does your mother hate herself?'

Jewish self-hate is a false-flag operation.

Leila Khaled is still out there: radical and alive.

§

While I waited for my bag on the luggage belt in Tel Aviv, I got a text marked urgent from my sister. Abigail the intellectual hotshot was now living in Brooklyn studying architecture.

They don't trust you over there, she texted. *Neither of them.*

Do you? I countered.

I looked up from my phone. The airport AC was blaring. Barbra smiled at me, wolflike.

Yeah, I trust that you'll run, my sister said, *if she tries to cut you again.*

My heart pounded with love. My mouth full of salty saliva. Barbra will not ever hurt me again. Barbra, self-loving, orphan of Operation Solomon. Barbra the Jewess, the keeper of knives.

Barbra, the first Beta Israel refusenik, took over the halls of Ben Gurion with ease. I forgot about the schmuck on the walkway behind her.

Here I was on her turf, in her thrall. Here, *we* were the *mistanenim*.

§

My mother always told the story like, 'You just walked off and didn't tell anyone.' My father said, 'It was your first incident of tail-chasing, kid.'

In Israel, on our family vacation right after my bar mitzvah, I remembered that Abigail had a whole-body heat rash. We were at the pool in the supposedly mixed neighbourhood and my mother was taking Abigail to the change rooms to put on some cream. My father was trying to fall asleep on his back on concrete. Girls here wore bathing suits that looked like pyjamas.

My father didn't want us to go to a public pool in Jaffa. He said we had a perfectly good one at the hotel.

My mother said, even way back then: 'Israel is like the Jim Crow American South.'

My father said, 'My God, Ruth, you exaggerate.'

'It is a fact,' my mother said. 'People have starting calling it apartheid.'

'And you don't think that is hyperbole? Jesus Christ in Jerusalem,' my father said.

This was the one mixed pool in Israel, according to my mother, where both Jewish and Arab families went to swim. 'Better than the Wailing Wall,' my mother said. She made us take public transit. '*Mein Gott*, let's just get in a cab,' my dad said.

'It's *one* bus. I think the kids can handle one bus.'

But Abigail whined the whole way there because she was too hot. Her forehead looked swollen. She had a towel around her neck.

'You should take that thing off your face,' I hissed down at her, holding the hand strap over my head.

I had the plush hotel towel in my bag. I'd started growing hair under my arms. I smelled everyone around me. My family stood out in Israel. Tourist Jews. The bus jerked way too fast through narrow streets. My father mouthed all the Hebrew words in the bus advertisements. My mother kept hunching over and straining to check the street signs out the window. I thought Abigail's forehead looked like there was water in it.

My mother suddenly rang the bell, stressed. 'This is it,' she said, corralling us. 'Come on, guys, this is us.'

There were no signs for the pool. My mother asked a few people, and Abigail really started to whine. My father kept asking if my mother should call the pool.

'You can't call a pool,' my mother said.

Then my father found this old man on the street who spoke Yiddish and he directed us to the *araber shvimmer*.

I sat crossed-legged on the edge of the cracked concrete deck by myself. Some girls swam in the deep end with their suits on like fins. When they climbed up the ladder, voluminous cloth sucked to their butts. The sun hit their dark fabric wrinkles. Glittering patches of black oil, rivulets. The Arab boys who were there wore normal swim shorts but the girls had to be all covered and suctioned. On one side of the pool there were a few Jewish girls suntanning in their bikinis and rubbing lotion on each other's thighs. Behind them was a line of old men on concrete benches with hairy chests and lit cigarettes.

I kept watching this one girl in the pool with really thick eyebrows and big breasts. She was covered in navy-blue volumes of spandex. Her head scarf slicked down the sides of her face. She saw me cross-legged with my surfer shorts. The girl's swaddled tits bounced in this strange slow-motion way in the water. I wondered what her hair looked like under there. She smiled at me. Her nipples were huge. I was trying not to look. I'd never seen a girl look like that in the water. I had to cover myself. Burning skin. She twirled in wide circles, fabric parting the pool. I knew she knew I was watching her as she danced. Oblivious, smiling, she bumped into one of the bikini-wearing girls in the pool. That girl yelled. It was crowded. I saw her pull on the dancing girl's spandex head scarf. My father lay flat, his mouth open with snores. My mother and Abigail had not returned from the change rooms. Then all of sudden, it was really sudden, the dancing girl smacked the bikini girl's face.

Then the dancing girl got swiftly pulled out of the pool by her armpits by some man in her family, I guessed. The Jewish girl in the bikini started crying. The dancing girl's mother was apoplectic. Little kids ran around them in water wings. People climbed out of the pool. The bikini girl wailed. The dancing girl put on her rubber bath shoes. Lifeguards or some kind of security guards appeared.

I stood up with both of my shoulders on fire. The dancing girl was being taken away. One of the security guards jumped into the pool. He had a *gun*. My father did not wake up. The kids in their water wings cried. The bikini girl was now being helped out of the pool. I looked backwards. The girl in the spandex bathing suit had disappeared.

I half-ran to the hall near the change rooms. I'd forgotten my sandals on deck. My shorts dripped. I pursued. The hallway was purplish and smelled of bare feet.

I spied the dancing girl and a woman going through rotary gates. The girl was hunched over. Her head scarf was off. She was being dragged by her bathing suit by the other woman. I got scared. I kept going, running through the windy tunnel to the pool entrance, too. I ducked underneath the turnstile. I followed them into the scorched parking lot. The girl had a swinging black braid and she was fighting the woman who was head-to-toe covered. Sun spiked my head from the open-faced sky. I thought of my sister. The girl being yanked. I thought, I cannot get back into this pool without cash. Then the woman pushed the girl up against the parking lot fence. I was scared. I crouched at the side of a car. The woman started slapping the side of the dancing girl's head. I burned my back on a gleaming door handle. The woman slapped the girl's head on repeat. I was paralyzed. That girl did not do anything wrong! Her elbows were up. She didn't make any sounds. A siren released from a speaker above me. The girl crumpled down at the fence. '*Stop!*' I heard myself say. My name came from the sky. 'Stop hitting her! Please!' My name on repeat. Her braid swinging around. I heard the voice of my mother, running in her bathing suit. A lifeguard was with her, a security guard.

'When I got back you weren't there!' my mother screamed at me, punching the hood of the car I'd been hiding behind. 'Your father was sleeping! We are *not* in Toronto! You *need* to tell me where you are!'

Cherry skin rippled out of her bathing-suit armpits.

I turned back around to the parking lot fence.

'My God, oh my God, look what happened to your feet.'

That hurt Arab girl and her mother were gone.

'Jesus Christ. This, your father has to see.'

Crooked blood lines between two of my toes. That girl had been slapped by her mother so hard. I hobbled back to the pool. My mother had spider-veined thighs. On deck, my father played war with my sister. Abigail's forehead glowed with zinc. My father wore mirrored sunglasses. He shook his head at me.

I noticed the bikinied girl and her friends sitting in a circle. The oiled-up, old, hairy bears had changed sides.

I hated my mother. I hated my father. I wiped the blood from my foot with a plush hotel towel. My mother sulked on the cracked concrete deck.

I thought, my mother did not know *where* I was because my mother did not know *who* I was.

In the pool's glare, in Israel, I felt like I'd just discovered my purpose in life.

My purpose was to help rescue kids from abuse. I thought of those kids on the monkey bars flying, the sad women dumped in the lot behind fences. My mother had said they were here from *domestic abuse*.

My thinking had progressed. Now it split off from my mom's.

I thought in a logically articulated sentence: I pledge to help kids who are being abused.

Look, Mom, now it's obvious to me that Barbra led me into what you call an *abusive dynamic* that by thirteen, in Israel, I'd already intuited existed.

I was not the victim; I was not the abuser.

I was fulfilling my fate of liberation, same as she.

§

I took Barbra's hand outside the airport as we waited for a cab. She'd changed from combat boots into strap-up-the-calf sandals. Our palms were sweating. It felt like a hundred degrees. I did not care what the schmuck thought of me and Barbra holding hands. She pulsed me in code. I pulsed her back. In Israel, it occurred to me, men were more in touch with their feelings. They could open right up – it was the flip side of fear. I felt it like a buzz – male passion, male emotion – in the air.

I imagined Ariane laughing: All this time you were a *Zionist*!

We got into a taxi. Barbra sat in the middle. The highway was jammed with tour buses, tanker trucks. We passed big-box malls next to highway huts. I kept pulsing her palm. I closed my eyes. My seven years without Barbra compressed into thought, this dizzying, totalizing, Zionist thought:

Sabbatai Zevi and Ka-Tzetnik are *interfacing*.

Multiple telephone wires hung low like intestines. I opened my eyes. The buildings were sand-coloured, semicircular.

I felt a crack in my lip. A horn on my head.

If possible check out the settlements, Abigail pinged me. *From a design POV: fucking blood-curdling!*

Our car descended from a highway down a thick concrete slope. The sun slid behind buildings marked with tar and graffiti. I wanted to glue myself onto Barbra's mushroom-cap shoulder. But I smelled rank. I got panicky.

I instinctively typed back to Abigail: *Pray for me.*

Look, I sort of knew and didn't know what was happening to me.

Of course we went to the Wailing Wall when me and Abigail were kids. I thought those Orthodox guys in their long grimy coats looked like black unicorns with those boxes on their heads.

'More like bogeymen,' Abigail said.

'That's the *Torah* in there.' My father acted offended. 'Tefillin is our sign to remember that God led us out of Egypt. It's like the airplane's black box; it's the *signal* of a Jew's devotion.'

We all watched the herd of black unicorns pitching back and forth on the spot.

My mother scoffed. 'Those ultra-religious always cheat on their wives.'

'Don't let them hear you say that.'

'Oooooh, shaking in my booties, look at me,' my mother said.

My mother made Abigail laugh.

I did not pack any pills. I forgot to pack my pills on purpose. I knew my breathing was laboured – extrinsic, mechanic. I pulsed Barbra's hand on repeat, on repeat.

Abigail wrote back: *WTF? Call Dad. Are u not ok?*

I manhandled my phone and shoved it away.

The road down here was stained with clouds of exhaust. Filipino families with strollers crossed the streets. It didn't seem like the beach was anywhere near. Smears of bird shit fell on open-toed feet. Crooked blood between toes, sandals twisted up legs.

Abbi, I thought, *I'm surrendering.*

'Home,' Barbra said. She took her hand away from me.

The schmuck was too silent. *Cuckoo* meant insane.

Then our cab stopped at the lights in front of a circular park. It was full of Black people standing around. Barbra roughly crawled over my lap.

'*Yo!*' she screamed out the window. 'This is where my Darfuri *bruhs* at!'

People waved at our taxi. Barbra yelled out their names. Her breasts over my head, her skirt in my face. At the far end of the park, I saw sun-drenched orange tents. Sheets flapping and hanging over a slide. Open boxes of fruit in the sun in a dry wading pool. An oversized cast-iron pot smoked on a grate.

The schmuck tapped my shoulder behind her. 'The rest of them are in Holot,' he said quietly. 'A concentration camp.'

Our taxi kept driving around the park. Barbra, exhilarated, returned to her place on the back seat.

In Israel, she'd said, *they treat us like dogs.*

Darfur was a place of genocide.

I remembered my Grade 7 teacher showing us slides of starving Ethiopian kids.

Operation Solomon was a miracle, my dad chanted.

Ka-Tzetnik was a diagnosed schizophrenic, Sugarman recounted.

For I have also been a stranger in a strange land, a voice landed.

'Are you okay?' Barbra said to me, dripping sweat.

I needed her hand. I found it again and I squeezed. She kept looking behind her through the rear window at all the people back there encamped. I thumbed *Holot* on my phone. *Open-air detention centre in the Negev,* it said. *Thousands of African asylum seekers have been sent to the prison. They have no life there. They are languishing.*

Suddenly I knew it was KZ, the Auschwitz survivor, who whispered in my ear: *See from where she was flung. See from whence she came.*

SZ, her old false Messiah, wanted in: *Jewish people know better, something must be done.*

KZ: *What is to be done?*

SZ: *Start from zero again.*

§

I did not think that Barbra would ever let Joel near her again after the time with GHB in the basement, but I just stood there and watched a second dog spray take place. He was rutting her in a ski mask in our fucking basement. It took me a second to piece it all together. This was a rape scene. A break-in. The sexual criminal broke into the foreign student's basement apartment and in this scene they have sex as if she is terrified. I could tell she was half-heartedly pushing him away. From her fake moans of terror, she was *directing* him.

'Call me a slut,' Barbra said under Joel's grimy, beige hand. *'International slut.'*

Before Sabbatai Zevi was imprisoned, he encouraged women to 'release their libidos' from the 'shackles of shame.' In the new world to come, everything was game.

'Slut. Jewish slut?' Joel laughed. 'That's what he calls you? I seriously don't get what you like about him.'

Me? Why the fuck was he talking about me?

'He's my friend,' Barbra slurred as Joel kept on bucking. 'I can say anything to him.'

Barbra had told me that she got suspended from school when she was thirteen years old because she punched a girl in the face who called her *kushi*. The principal of the school told Barbra it was *her* fault. The girl lost a tooth. Blood spurted from her mouth. The principal said that Barbra had to work harder to be 'good.'

'What about high school? Was it different?'

'Yeah,' Barbra said. 'Because I had tits and ass then!'

'But what about the other Ethiopian kids?' I continued. 'Why didn't you guys band together? Challenge things?'

'You can't intellectualize your childhood,' she said.

By the end of the summer, I realized that Barbra was not ever an actress-in-training. She *directed* things.

And I realized that Sabbatai Zevi's recognition of female power had been completely paved over in Judaism for me. Until I met the Ethiopian-Israeli orphan, Judaism was all stodgy, male-led, rule-abiding.

Joel had his hands around Barbra's neck. He kept trying to kiss her and she kept spitting at him. He fucked like a sprinter. Barbra started hyperventilating.

My teeth touched each other in my mouth like sheet metal. I stomped my feet in the army boots.

'Mother*fuck*er. You said he wasn't here.'

Barbra looked at me, flushed. Joel yanked up his shorts.

It occurred to me that Sabbatai Zevi's upside-down behaviour in Judaism was, in fact, just egalitarianism.

Barbra stayed on her back on her bed in the basement.

I went up to the kitchen and made myself ramen.

I heard Joel leave a few minutes later through our side door.

I burned my tongue. Female prophets. She put blood in the broth.

§

Our taxi stopped in front of a row of massive, grille-windowed buildings. Bedsheets and pyjamas flapped from balcony bars. This was what I imagined buildings looked like in Poland – communist, endless, grey cement blocks.

One stunted, fungal palm tree grew on a mound of dry grass.

Schmuck paid the driver. I got our bags from the trunk. The wet wind engulfed me as I watched her walk toward one building, holding down her skirt. To a building with seven gold Hebrew letters etched in the door glass.

KZ feels good in the house, the survivor said in my head.

In the lobby of the building, a bamboo-lily fan beat. A group of grizzled middle-aged men played dice around a kidney-shaped coffee table. The floor was rubber, checkered black-and-white. This place felt like Florida and Poland and Addis Ababa.

Barbra waltzed through the lobby. The schmuck greeted the gamblers. A sign on the wall read *No Guests After 10.*

'There's a barber on the seventh,' Barbra said, opening a door to the stairs. 'And a club where we watch films. You can get a cheap phone on the ninth or the tenth.'

I did not need any phone. I needed to fuck her.

Go easy, warned KZ. *Tread carefully.*

I followed Barbra into the stairwell. The schmuck trailed behind me. It smelled in this stairwell like the residue of meat. I wanted him gone. I knew she wanted him gone, too. Even my father wanted him gone.

That kind of want may be falsehood, interjected SZ.

I saw ink on her fingers. She slashed the wall as she climbed.

'Don't worry, not the penthouse,' Barbra laughed as if everything were fine.

Careful, KZ whispered. *She'll take everything in your mind.*

SZ: *Golden shackles are still shackles.*

KZ: *Baruch Hashem.*

I looked way up in the hallway. I had a backload of sweat. I saw Barbra's L-shaped bare legs high up through a grate. She exited the stairwell. The schmuck sprinted behind me. Rosy panties. Jewish girl. Jezebel. I continued to climb.

It was stuffy inside the fourteenth-floor hallway. An old air conditioner was lodged at the end of the hall underneath a cloudy, pentagon-shaped stained glass. My heart beat rapidly. I needed to concentrate. Barbra waved at me from an open door. The schmuck lingered in the hallway like a turtle, duffle bag on his back. He lit up that same South American pipe. I glanced upward at the prickly beige stucco ceiling. That pentagon-shaped window was soldered shut. In this high-rise, I realized, there were no fire alarms. I heard radio static, plates cracking, a human rasp. I shuffled forward, swatting the schmuck's smoke from my face.

KZ: *A man cannot fight another man when he's weak.*

SZ: *Men need to join arms or just lie down to die.*

KZ: *You know, that's offensive in this context. We did not go like sheep to the slaughter.*

SZ: *Sorry, my brother, I don't mean to cause harm.*

I wanted to smash the schmuck out of her system.

He reached out his arm to me: *H'bayit shli, oo h'bayit shlach.*

Horror is a planet, KZ whispered. *We live in its system.*

SZ: *You must wander through horror to rescue what is good there.*

KZ: *I will if you do.*

SZ: *Let's go in and see.*

I could not plug my ears to the voices.

KZ: *A hereafter that's not here and not after.*

SZ: *Jew-boy, we're glad you understand.*

I entered a little hotel room for a good-girl model orphan. I saw a dome-shaped silver headboard behind a pink king-sized bed. The silver-domed headboard was embedded with hooks. Rubber pulleys looped from those hooks up to hooks in the ceiling. The ceiling was the same as in the hallway: spiky dirty beige.

I felt angry. I felt trapped. An outmoded cockroach. Why'd she lure me up here again?

KZ: *Shhh, man, shhhh. Stem your rage.*

SZ: *You have to stay cool or they'll lock you away.*

My first thought: *She'd been attached to that thing.*

My next thought: *The schmuck was the head of a sex-trafficking ring.*

My third: *That metallic, hooked headboard was his system of abuse.*

'Welcome to my pad,' Barbra said. 'Let me get you a drink.'

My bag dropped on the ash-coloured carpet.

KZ: *Don't let her get the upper hand.*

SZ: *From orphan girls, thy fruit is found.*

In this fourteenth-floor pad, it occurred to me that I'd been *duped*. Barbra and the schmuck practised straight-up, military-grade s/m! He was her *pimp*. I wanted to die. I wished I'd been brainwashed in Toronto like all the JSA men.

Relax a little, KZ counselled.

SZ: *See if you can melt into the feminine, man.*

'No!' I blurted.

The schmuck looked at me and laughed.

'Who *is* he?' I yelled. 'Tell me, is he's your fucking pimp?'

'You came all the way here to ask me *this*?' Barbra said.

Wrong move, we told you, scolded KZ.

SZ: *Yeah, you gotta stop with the hatred of whoredom, my friend.*

Hot teardrops trickled down from my armpits. One oblong-shaped window cut to the acid-blue sky. I squeezed my eyes shut. I reopened them. Beside that bed were shelves filled with books and cups and magazines.

'Relax,' Barbra whispered, staring at me.

I tried to take stock of the situation. That silver hooked headboard wrecked my peripheral vision.

Barbra handed me a glass of red wine in a disposable cup. I watched her strut to the window and open it with one arm. I saw the sheen of her neck hairs. The chemical field of the sky. Her dipped spine and ass underneath the potato-sack dress. I wanted to see her bend over and spread. I wanted to pull up that dress. I wanted to pull down her panties and fuck her.

Is this really what you came here for? my mother said.

He was summoned, said KZ in my defence.

SZ: *The Queen helps all Jew-boys get their bearings, get ahead.*

I was scared of myself. Scared of pushing her out.

'I need to find a hostel,' I rasped. 'Just somewhere to sleep.'

Barbra spun around, spilling wine on the floor. 'But you just got here. We haven't even started yet!'

I had a wrecked gut and a bad case of the voices.

'I need to go, I need to feel better,' I said.

Barbra came at me. I really did not want her to see me like this. I needed my bearings. I needed my meds. I did not want to be here with her and him. But Barbra kept coming at me, arms open, and led me like Lot to the furry bedspread.

'*Please*,' she whispered, leaning in to my ear. 'Remember what I said?'

When? At home? Did she mean her real name?

KZ: *Women only tell the truth in their prison diaries.*

SZ: *Women shall lead us to a place of no more wandering.*

The Queen of Sheba didn't get anywhere with King Solomon. Ka-Tzetnik died of starvation, alone. Sabhatai Zevi languished in prison. Darfuris in limbo. Leila Khaled will not return. God, I had to get out of this fourteenth-floor chamber. I forced myself out of her slippery hands. I evaded the bed where he frigidly lay. I launched myself backwards at the door, centrifugal, scuttling.

'Don't let him leave!'

The schmuck leapt up at me, military-style. The first thing I saw was his belt-buckle flint.

'Get the fuck off me, man! Tell him to stop it!' I screamed.

I felt his breath toxic, excited. He liked being rough. Queen watched as the schmuck bound my wrists with duct tape, black sheen.

§

On top of the mountain, strapped up to the headboard, my eyes stayed on the knife they kept passing between them. My mouth had been taped, my hands pulled to the ceiling. I was strung up to the dome, tied with the pulleys. Her knife had a rust-coloured edge, a carved wooden handle. I watched her, squint-eyed. Last rays of red sun filtered in. I remembered her, half-naked, smashed in my old room. Barbra, teenager. I'd sucked on her tits. The headboard felt medical on my bare ass.

KZ: *We got your back, bruh.*

SZ: *Chin up, follow through.*

Spit bubbled and pooled behind the duct tape. I thought, if she was in charge, she wouldn't hurt me again.

Reality and phantasm, gurgled KZ, *they're the same.*

SZ: *Yeah, dread and hope – plus a little nooky – fuels all stories. Please, you guys, stop distracting me!*

I tried, as her captive, to memorize her face. Sleek spherical forehead, cat tongue on her lip. Lips rubbing together, her stern way of being. I stared at the titles of the books on her shelves. Most were Hebrew, but one pile in English had Krasznahorkai, Hoffman, and Shishkin.

The ceiling buckled at the light fixture like it was holding hot water. The only door out of this room had been locked and bolt-chained. Fourteen floors up in this ancient apartment. Barbra paced in her sack dress, scratching her arms. I wholly believed she would not hurt me again.

KZ: *But everyone, bruh, undergoes suffering.*

Seven years ago, after I was taken to the hospital, Barbra showed the police her cut-up left breast. Barbra told the police that she was afraid. Barbra called my mother in Portland to say I'd abused her. I had to confess our knife play to the cops.

'God, what did I teach you? Did I not teach you? You can't take your stuff out on a girl!' cried my mom.

I shook my head in my hospital bed. *That was not what happened!*

My mother couldn't look at me. She did not believe me.

I bubbled spit into my tape. Barbra took off her rose-coloured sack. I felt my cock pulse. She had on a black bra and pink panties. I wanted to suck on everything.

I got seventeen stitches in the hospital that night.

I heard myself breathing sloppily like a dog. I was constricted. I did not understand to what I'd consented.

Was I here for a modern-day Jew-boy sacrifice?

Absolutely not! KZ and SZ said in unison.

The schmuck stepped up onto the bed. Mothball groin hit my face. My father told me not to come here. I gagged. My father begged me. Mattress softened. The schmuck cranked my body up higher with rubber. Arms straight upraised, elbows locked with his furor. I felt army pants, gristle. I needed to breathe. The schmuck picked the tape off with his fingernail from my face.

'Fuck you,' was the first thing I said.

Tell him where to go, KZ applauded.

SZ: *Smash oppressors the world over.*

KZ: *So hatred has no place.*

Now Barbra entered the picture, shushing and slicking back hairs from my head. Where was the knife now? What was she doing instead? I felt doe-eyed. The schmuck jumped off of the bed. Barbra kept trying to soothe me. I knew they were both prepping me for sacrifice, for death.

KZ: *Reject it.*

SZ: *Rejoice it.*

'Trust me,' Barbra said. She kept stroking my forehead and oiling down my thick hairs with her sweat.

I did not feel soothed. I was scared of the blade.

The end of the line for Ka-Tzetnik was that his wife made him do a shitload of drugs. 'My guy' could not heal. He burned all his books.

'Don't kill me,' I wept.

My eyes bulged like jewels. I wailed. A bitch. Barbra licked my cheek, so I turned my head. Her mouth was right there and she sucked out my tongue. The schmuck was watching. Barbra slid two fingers in my mouth. She grabbed on to my tongue. Then she coated my groin with both our spit. Bigger than the dome. Cold as a fridge. This was a snuff scene. A saggy grey web suffocated my face.

'Take me down now,' I panted, totally freaked.

'Beg harder, Jew-boy.'

'Take me down, Barbra. *Please!*'

God, how many times had I finished our story in my head? What if that knife had been one fraction higher?

The web stuffed my nostrils. It wrapped round my throat. I felt the schmuck's cock in his army-pant tent. Barbra glanced backwards at him, squeezing me.

'I want to hear you *really* scared.'

Knife near. Suicide is done in the wrists.

'I can't feel my arms! I swear I can't feel them!'

'Like that. Good boy.'

My cock was in her hands. God, where was the knife? KZ and SZ were silent for a second. Point up. No more voices. I felt lightning in my body, then a short, brutal nick. I screamed. I shot cum right into her fist. It felt like a heart attack, but when I looked down, I saw nothing had erupted. Mock orgasm.

KZ and SZ started hysterically laughing.

The sun had gone grey. I heard myself panting wet.

'Now,' Barbra ordered, her voice grisly again.

In slow motion I watched him hand her the knife.

'God, I don't want to die here, please, I don't want to die!'

She was humming some prayer. He was watching me squeal. Her face near my cock, bobbing. Tears at the head.

Soap bubbles' glint. Her wolflike saliva. Even my asshole started to beat.

'God, let me *live*, fuck, I'm begging you, please…'

My spine jerked on the headboard. My cock shrivelled backwards. I banged myself, rag doll.

SZ: *The lamb shall be spared.*

'Please, God, save me!'

The blade was the length of my tongue from its root.

KZ: *I wish to hell that we had been believed.*

'*Baruch atah adonai*,' Barbra started.

I think I blacked out. I think I came to.

My tongue grew some fungus. Fungus makes you schizophrenic.

The Queen of Sheba travelled for twenty-four days from Addis Ababa to Jerusalem. She came bearing gifts, wearing jewels, her skin tantalizing. The glorious six-foot-tall African queen wanted King Solomon to love her and worship her, and Solomon did, even though he had two hundred wives.

Barbra slid up me, glossy. Her boobs were cold and bulblike.

'I did it,' she said. 'Now you're like me.'

Elephantitis of my groin. Ballooning, beating, swollen head. It felt like honey. Mucky. Every part of me rank. The Queen of Sheba fucked with Solomon's mind. The Queen of Sheba introduced fucking with the mind.

The knife lay on the shelf on the top of her books.

Barbra was a circumciser. I'd just converted to a Hebrew female system.

The system of the Black Hebrew female circumciser had returned.

I smiled. I can't help you. A new fucking thesis.

Barbra said, 'See?'

The first circumciser in the Bible was Tzipporah. Her name was Tzipporah. I'd call her TZ. I imagined us here in this room for the rest of our lives. The euphoric rotunda. TZ unhooked me from the headboard. All systems of abuse had been deactivated. Now even the schmuck seemed quiet and fine. Heat returned to my arms. I heard myself laughing. I curled up like a kid at her silver-domed headboard. I didn't care who was watching. I felt so nice in a stream. A stream that was pulsing and oscillating.

§

My mother had already been gone for a week when my father took us downtown for Chinese.

'She'll come back,' my father said, maudlin, sucking a rib. 'When you've been together as long as we have, anything can work.'

I didn't know if my father actually believed that my mom was coming back. She had a really good job. She'd taken my sister. The end of the summer was nigh.

'One thing Israel doesn't have is Chinatown,' my father said, mouth full, passing the pea shoots to Barbra. 'Eat up, guys. Come on. You should eat.'

Barbra seemed distracted. She pulverized rice with a fork at the rim of her plate. My father had ordered too much for three people.

'In Chinatown, we suspend the dietary laws,' My father said, laughing, wiping sauce from his chin. 'Pork is kosher south of Bloor.'

'You know I don't eat pig,' Barbra said.

My father stopped laughing. My lips dripped chili oil. Barbra, I saw, had a twitch in her cheek.

My father pushed away from the table. 'Yep. Just a trip to the men's room,' he said.

I was embarrassed. 50 Cent sang 'In da Club.' Barbra reached for my thigh under the tablecloth and squeezed.

'Get him to go to the liquor store,' she said.

'We have enough.'

'Well, I need more for tomorrow.'

I took a deep breath. 'Look, my dad's just not used to being challenged, okay?'

'I didn't challenge him.'

'Yeah, you did. That's what you do.'

Barbra twitched. 'All I said was *no fucking pig*.'

I was still angry about what she did with Joel.

'Look, my father was just trying to tell you why he wasn't kosher, all right? You need to stop pushing. You need to step down.'

For the first time since she entered our house, I felt hate. I thought that supplying her with wine would keep her off drugs. But how many fucking bottles did she need? How much did she have to split herself apart and put herself back together? Fuck, I'd followed everything she'd wanted for nearly eight weeks! I'd scratched her back, played her games, asked my dad for all kinds of shit. My dad got her a *visa*. She didn't know how much we'd done. And what'd she do for me? She fucked my best friend.

The paramedics landed in the restaurant like troops. They put rings on my arms, a can on my neck. I heard Barbra screaming but I could not see. The plastic tablecloth wrinkles.

No limit to the ceiling. What I remembered was her hand in my hair. Slow-motion scuffle under the tablecloth skirt. It was her fist, then her hand holding me up by the scruff.

'Can you feel this?' the paramedics asked me, pushing.

Barbra, doe-eyed model orphan, had taken the horns.

I had a can on my neck. I could only feel pressure.

'Take it easy, kid. *Breathe.*'

I knew the summer would not go on forever.

'What's your name? Does he know his name?'

Jew-boy was my given name.

'He's in shock. He needs oxygen.'

Chili oil was demonic. Barbra had brought us some kind of new blade.

'Take a breath now,' they said. 'Try to tell us your name.'

She'd stood up from the table underneath the tablecloth skirt. She had a left hand, a left fist. I thought she was looking for my father. All I thought was: we are taking a break. My father had been gone for too long in the bathroom. I saw the gleam for one second under her skirt. It was curved, leather-sheathed. It had all these grey teeth.

'She got kicked out of the army. Does that not concern you?' my mother shrieked.

I felt gurgling, no air. Her left fist in my hair. Charred beef. Ice-cold smoke.

Abigail cried on the phone. She kept saying she missed me. She *missed* me.

The knife at my neck was when the first woman screamed.

My sounds ricocheted off the restaurant wall. Abduction by force. My neck was a puppet. Abduction was *always* by violent force. Where was my father? Barbra overtaken. Her head was measured and sprayed with DDT. My mother had not wanted her to come to our home in the first place. Kafka wrote that his mother in their family was like the 'beater in the hunt.' He meant that the mother was the one who chased the birds into violence. The mother was the one who *found* the violence, in fact, the one who prepped all those birds for the eager shotgun. Cheap wine covered up trauma. Beef upturned on the carpet. I heard a high-pitched, hovering, whimpering wind.

'Those ISIS guys are evil,' my father said. 'They kill the Jews and Japanese.'

I thought, mothers are beaters and visionaries.

My neck, the fountain. Blood hit the plastic. Barbra jiggled the knife. My phlegm built a poultice. I begged my dad to come back. I prayed to him, *Dad, rescue me.*

At the hospital later, my father appeared. He was bloodless, pacing, on the phone with my mom. When I opened my eyes again, she was there right with me.

'She's being deported,' my mother whispered, lips droopy.

Later, somewhere at the foot of my cot, I heard Bornstein pronouncing in stone to my parents: Lucky she was too drunk to find the jugular vein.

§

I could piss even though I was tender and swollen. There was one tiny nick. It just felt like a stitch. Some lump that slid near the back rim of my dick.

Take yourself to a hospital, Jesus Christ! my father yelled.

Self-care is the boot of female power, my mother said.

Radio silence from my two mystical buddies.

Barbra and I were now completely in sync.

And there was that other voice now. I called her TZ. The uncircumciser, the perverted survivor, the refusenik, my reinstated queen.

Barbra handed me a pair of white harem pants. She already had on a pair of her own. We were both garbed all in white. Loose pants, no pain. It was the middle of the night, three hours from dawn.

The schmuck was stretched out under the sheets like a corpse. He'd fallen asleep while I was examining myself in the john. Barbra searched through her purse and the schmuck's army pants. Her whole face was slick. Sweat dripped down her temples. She pocketed a wad of his shekels. She gave me the knife from on top of her books.

'He won't follow us,' Barbra whispered. 'Take it. Then we're done.'

Barbra shook the blade at me, blurry.

'I don't understand.'

'Snuff him out, man,' she whispered. 'This is what I need done.'

Barbra eyed me, musk pouring, knife out to his body. Smeared hotel walls. A bad man on the bed. I was nicked. I got lucid. This was a new kind of thinking, not hermetically sealed. TZ had cut me symbolically in order to let real thoughts in. I thought of hoisting his corpse out of the pentagon window. False flag, palm tree, my unfettered head.

The knife dripped in my hand like an elephant's tusk. We were both pouring sweat, no air in this box. But the window was open. She planted the handle. My soiled hand grasped it. The uncircumciser's blade.

One flappy arm glued over both the schmuck's eyes. His

grey dick under there, a stunt bat, a problem. Her silvery hooked headboard loomed to my left.

'Do it,' she whispered.

Cold in my harem drop crotch. The knife slipped in my squeeze.

'I can't. I can't do it.'

'Yes, you can do anything.'

SZ said KZ returned: *Bruh, this is re-happening.*

There was no easy fix. The whole world is backwards. Persecution endures, persecution remains. She was behind me all slick, needling into my back.

'He's my captor,' she whispered. 'He's tormented me.'

I saw her in my living room, goose-flesh tongue on slimy white neck. Anointed in musk. Submissive, seductive. *Do it* was her anthem. *Undo* was hers, too.

I plunged the knife down once into his thigh. It was chicken meat. In-out. Schmuck jerked like a board. I hit a vein. His eyes glistened. I let the blade free. Blood spurted out in an arc. In-out. His legs were meat. I stared at the slit that I'd made. The schmuck yanked a rubber pulley from the headboard. He started tourniqueting.

Somehow she was running us out of the room. Somehow my legs moved. Christof was awake. I kept feeling the plunge. Like a mother banging meat. In-out. There was gristle. Bare bulbs. My mouth felt like wallpaper glue. I was attached to her jog in the hallway. We thumped down the stairwell, each floor another rung.

His rust-coloured spray stained our white-coloured sacks.

TZ's arm helped me through the underground garage. The place was blue-lit with cylindrical posts. Outside the chamber, buses sat dead in a chain. It wasn't dawn yet, no cracks happening.

§

Sugarman had tried to teach me that Ka-Tzetnik 135633 and all survivors write down their memories through the sieve of their trauma.

On the witness stand at Adolf Eichmann's trial in Jerusalem, Ka-Tzetnik the writer-survivor was called to testify. But he could not complete his testimony because he started convulsing. KZ convulsed with the knowledge that *he* could have been Eichmann. Convulsing, discounted, Ka-Tzetnik had to be taken away.

What the writer-survivor was trying to say to his brethren was: I was *he* and he was *me*.

Sabbatai Zevi, if he'd been there, would have agreed.

TZ: *No more desecration. No more violation. Release us all from persecution.*

Buruk New, Ameyn.

§

We walked to the park in the darkness. The earth was so quiet. About seven tents blistered in the rusted playground.

'They know me here,' whispered Barbra. 'This is where we'll sleep.'

She led me through garbage bags and rotting boxes of fruit.

I lay on my back on the lukewarm cement.

Barbra sat near me, crossed-legged. 'Hey,' she whispered. 'It's okay.'

I inched my head into the space of her burning-hot lap. I kept flinching. Alien. I could not rest. I kept feeling the plunge. People go mute from horror. I remembered how Abigail used to watch movies like *The Texas Chainsaw Massacre* and all the *Halloweens*. She said it was because then she would *know* that a man would actually kill her – she could beg and beg and it wouldn't matter to him. But I felt that night in Barbra's lap in the park, with my light-bulb-shaped head and blood-splattered pants, I thought that girls in horror movies were maybe not a reliable form of thinking. Or maybe Abigail was right, they were the pinnacle of thinking. Girls in horror films knew exactly how to think, how to act, how to be.

'Barbra, I got you wrong,' I moaned.

I don't know if my words came out clear or garbled. It felt muddy inside the no pills in my head.

'I'm sorry.'

I tried to make my head smaller. I made it so small for one second that she slid away and left me there.

Through a blur, I watched her walk through the park. She walked to one man who stood underneath a lamplight. I watched them together. They were exactly the same height.

When Barbra returned sometime later, she held two cups of coffee. 'Mutasim said I could stay. Join the fight.'

I scalded the roof of my mouth. My thoughts felt parodic. I mean, they parroted hers. I agreed: she should stay, she should fight. They were planning a protest. They would branch out and fight in the south and the west. Here was her home now. A new place, restless.

'I'm sorry,' I repeated. 'I got you all wrong.'

'Bruh,' Barbra whispered, 'you were my stepping stone.'

I remembered her swan's neck on my pillow. I remembered each time she graced my bed. The X-acto. The stopping. The wine to help thinking.

'Barbra,' I croaked.

She leaned toward my elephant face. She kissed me. I choked. It burned in my memory.

This was a park full of humans in need. What was needed from me now was only to leave.

For a few more hours, I lay in a tent blasted with sun. My mouth was covered with crust. It hurt everywhere. I already missed her. I heard her outside the tent with the others, near where garments were hung.

I crawled out at noon like the bug that I was. I'd be starting from zero. I'd be tracking backwards. Seven years ago, what made me think that I knew?

Barbra, shining, twelve feet tall. The survivor who knows there are no forsaken human beings.

§

I see Divine Presence ablaze in the dark of the block, wrote Ka-Tzetnik. *I am my own cortège; I am behind my own bumping head.*

§

Abigail sat with me on the L-shaped leather couch. My dad was in Florida for a week with his 'woman friend.'

'What does that mean?' I asked my sister. 'Is he getting remarried?'

'If he does we'll be his flower girls,' Abigail snorted.

Me and my sister clinked glasses full of cheapskate red wine. Abigail had cooked us some kind of soup with kidney beans.

Abigail had blossomed. I knew that word was disgusting. But I just mean she'd become this vital human being.

'I told Dad I'd remind you to take your medication,' she said.

I rolled my eyes. She was also a pawn for parental reasons.

'I know that there is no perfect treatment for schizoaffective disorder,' Abigail said, taking a deep breath. 'We know that it afflicts people of all ages, all races, across gender and class lines, we know that there is not one accepted or agreed-upon method of treatment, pharmaceutically or therapeutically speaking.'

'No such thing as a clean exit wound.' I looked at my sister. I slurped the soup she had made.

'She meddled with you. I'll give them that. And for that I'll never forgive her,' Abigail said. 'But I can accept that that's just me and how I go about things.'

As me and my sister at home drank the same wine that she drank, Barbra remained by the fire in the refugee camp.

Abigail said, 'When people divorce – which I can totally understand in Mom and Dad's case – you are supposed to keep the siblings together. That's not rocket science. Me and you should've been on planes together. We should've had a schedule, we should've had vacations at the same time. Instead, look what happened, I didn't know who you became. And you ignored me, too. Seven years is a really long time.

'Mom always told me that you had a "mental condition." She always said it was good that I was out of the house for all of high school so that there was no, I don't know, contamination? Look, it wouldn't surprise me if she used that word, okay? Basically, she didn't want you to influence me. Which is totally fucked. They are two educated people who both seriously somehow thought that mental illness was contagious.'

'I don't know,' I said. 'I think they just didn't want it for me.'

I thought of a good working family slogan: *Bruh's in your broth.*

'Look, sometimes,' Abigail said, 'when I came back to visit you and Dad, you just seemed completely normal to me. Like, you were always reading. You were in school. You had girls over almost every night in the basement. And when you started going out with Ariane, I thought, how can he have a serious "mental condition" if he's going out with *her*? Ariane was so fucking smart, she was hot, I liked her so much. But Mom just kept telling me to be careful, to leave you alone. She kept saying, "He's not the kid I raised."

'I'm sorry,' my sister continued. 'I'm just telling you, for seven years, I did not really know what to believe.'

My mother's vision was making me distressed. I did not like my sister's version of the story either. I wiped my face. I put down the soup.

'Look,' Abigail said quietly. 'I'm angry at them. I'm happy to be right here now, with you.'

Heat swelled into the back of my throat.

'Like, they both mourn some sort of "good son no more," which is trash, in my opinion. Both of them somehow think that *she* was the force that triggered your "change."'

I nodded in silence. My heat smouldered and spread.

'And I've broken it to them in words that they can understand: no one is able to trigger a mental disorder. It's *no one*'s fucking fault. Schizoaffective is *pre-existing*.'

Trying to swallow, I regarded my sister. Pre-existing forking is the ability to think.

KZ: *If you see a boundary, cross it, cross through to the other side.*

SZ: *Because that's what God does, just like the perverts.*

TZ: *God mixes God-self with the unjust stink of things.*

After Abigail left and went back to New York and after my dad returned with his lady friend and after my West Coast mother who I talked to every day had been revealed as a little unreliable, I wandered the streets where we all used to live. I noticed the sidewalks were degraded. The roads had bullet-sized cracks. I realized that the bagel stores were all run by Filipino Catholics. I refilled my prescriptions in New Age Jewish wellness digs.

I felt like a bite had been taken out of me.

So I nurtured TZ's voice as a secret entity.

Books Cited

Franz Kafka, *Letter to the Father* (Schocken, 2015).

———. *The Metamorphosis* (W.W. Norton, 2014).

Gershom Scholem, *Sabbatai Sevi: The Mystical Messiah* (Princeton University Press, 1973).

Ka-Tzetnik 135633, *House of Dolls* (Panther Books, 1958).

———, *Shvitti* (First Gateways, 1988).

Also noted:

Ruth Franklin, *A Thousand Darknesses: Lies and Truth in Holocaust Fiction* (Oxford University Press, 2013).

Sander Gilman, *The Jew's Body* (Routledge, 1991).

Mya Guarnieri Jaradat, *The Unchosen: The Lives of Israel's New Others* (Pluto Press, 2017).

Franz Kafka, *Amerika: The Missing Person* (Schocken, 2011).

Leila Khaled (as told to George Hajjar), *My People Shall Live: Autobiography of a Revolutionary* (New Canada Publications, 1975).

Ilan Pappe, *The Ethnic Cleansing of Palestine* (Oneworld Publications, 2007).

Ida Rapoport-Albert, *Women and the Messianic Heresy of Sabbatai Zevi, 1666-1816* (The Littman Library of Jewish Civilization, 2015).

Élisabeth Roudinesco, *Our Dark Side: A History of Perversion* (Polity Press, 2009).

Idith Zertal, *Israel's Holocaust and the Politics of Nationhood* (Cambridge University Press, 2010).

Tamara Faith Berger was born in Toronto. She published her first book, *Lie with Me*, in 1999, and it was made into a film in 2004. In 2001, *A Woman Alone at Night* was published. These two novels were collected in *Little Cat*. Her third book, *Maidenhead*, won the 2012 Believer Book Award. She is also the author of *Kuntalini* and is writing for film and television.

Thank you: Clement Virgo, Wolf Virgo, Alana Wilson, Martha Webb, Rosa Pagano, Ariane Cruz, Anakana Schofield, Rena Zimmerman, Stuart Ross, Allen Forbes, Nancy Lee.

Typeset in Albertina

Printed at the Coach House on bpNichol Lane in Toronto, Ontario, on
Zephyr Antique Laid paper, which was manufactured, acid-free, in
Saint-Jérôme, Quebec, from second-growth forests. This book was
printed with vegetable-based ink on a 1973 Heidelberg KORD offset
litho press. Its pages were folded on a Baumfolder, gathered by hand,
bound on a Sulby Auto-Minabinda and trimmed on a Polar single-
knife cutter.

Edited and designed by Alana Wilcox
Cover by Ingrid Paulson
Author photo by Yuula Benivolski

Coach House Books
80 bpNichol Lane
Toronto ON M5S 3J4
Canada

416 979 2217
800 367 6360

mail@chbooks.com
www.chbooks.com